LOVED BY A DRAGON

Fallen Immortals 7

ALISA WOODS

Cover Design by Steven Novak

ISBN-13: 9798869394590

Chapter One

Erelah sent the thought to Leksander's mind then banked hard to the right—she'd caught the foul, sulfurous stench of demon, *Odious Class,* and her body instinctively followed, as was right for any angeling worth her wings. She trusted Leksander to follow her lead, if not outright scent the demon himself. She dipped down to skim the towers of Seattle, and soon enough, the moonlight gleamed on Leksander's silver scales beside her.

What do you know about shifter bars? His thoughts pushed into her mind, mocking her. They must speak this way due to their forms—he in his royal dragon of the House of Smoke, she with her angel wings put to purpose—but she did not care for it. Too much was said or implied or felt that would be better left alone.

I read the human news. She kept most of her irritation in her own mind.

He still laughed. His dragon teeth—beautifully sharp and long and white—were made even more luminescent by the moon. Not as entrancing or powerful as an angel blade, but close. She loved their fierceness in the service of protecting humanity… less so when small tendrils of blue dragonfire curled around them as he huffed out laughter directed at her.

She scowled. *The bars are a good suggestion.* Then she banked again and dipped still lower, now weaving through the urban canyons of the city. The hunt enlivened her blood, and her whole body tingled with anticipation. The night air rushed over her skin, cooling the ever-present heat of her angel half. She'd worn a lightweight toga for their hunt, but it was a poor choice—the top was bare enough and clung well to her body, but the trailing fabric flapped in the wind and slowed her down. Next time, she would find something without loose pieces.

Leksander caught up to her again.

She could easily outrun him, but they were working together. She slowed her pace.

I'm not going to find a mate in a bar. Leksander's humor had tempered, and he was being serious now. Good. She couldn't understand why he refused to pursue his duty with all the ardency and fervor it warranted. He knew the stakes. All of humanity's safety from the infernal fae, not to mention the demons they were hunting, depended on the House of Smoke renewing the treaty for another five hundred years. The other two princes had managed to find a mate and produce a dragonling, although she would never understand why they made such a difficulty of it. Now it was Leksander's turn, and he could no longer shirk his duty. Yet, he continued to argue with her, this third night running, and her patience was wearing thin.

Patience was a Virtue, one every angeling should culti-vate, along with the other six. But Erelah's faction was Chastity. That was her strength… the rest were an effort.

Her powerful white wings cut the air, pulling her to a

stop mid-flight and hovering her above the alleyway where the demon lurked. It had infested a poor man who by the sad state of his attire lived on the streets. Evil preyed most often on the weakest, most vulnerable of humanity's precious children. His fragile state made the man's possession all the more vile. Her angel power pulsed, and the heat of it sizzled her blood—she ached to slay that demon, but she had a point to make to Leksander first.

He drew to a stop next to her, his long tail just brushing the rooftops below.

A bar is a perfectly reasonable place to find a mate, Erelah pressed. *All manner of human women frequent them, lusting precisely for men who are shifters. Sex occurs right there, in the bar. You should have immediate knowledge of whether love is possible. If not, there are many others already there, just waiting for you to—*

Erelah! He was inexplicably irritated. *I'm not going to sleep my way through Seattle's bars—*

Why not? She winged closer to him, still hovering above the alley. The demon called to her, but she ignored it. This was more important. *I do not understand this, Leksander. You know your duty! Why do you not take an obvious opportunity to—*

I need no reminder of my duty. The silver in his eyes flashed, and his tail flicked.

She drew her blade from its holster, which was strapped to her thigh and barely hidden by the thin wrappings of her toga. Then she glared at Leksander. If she thought a good battle would shake the stubbornness from his head... but she couldn't chance it. She might work to embrace her Virtues via bouts with other angelings, but she could not hurt *them,* not seriously. Their blades and powers were evenly matched—it would take a Seraphim's blade or a shadow angel's tricks to draw blood from an angeling. But Leksander was all too vulnerable. He was human, yes, but both of his parents had been dragon, an unusual arrangement that left him stronger than most. Plus his royal lineage meant a large dose of summer fae magic pulsed in his veins, something that caused a constant, slightly irritating hum in her mind whenever he was near. Her blade wouldn't harm the human part, but it would outright slay the dragon and fae within him. Leksander was her friend, his House an ally to all angelkind, but his very nature was a rebuke to everything on the light side. Lucifer himself, the most powerful of the dark archangels, took dragon form during the Fall. Yet, Erelah would never raise her blade to Leksander, simply because protecting humanity was her highest duty, and Leksander and all his House played the most important of roles in that.

The demon on the other hand…

She flipped the blade to an overhand grip and dove into the alley below.

This—*demon slaying*—was what she was made for.

She was a *Protector Class* angeling, but she still managed a decent warrior cry. Her blade held high, she dropped down on the man and the vile demon that writhed within him, plunging the blade with a solid *thunk* into his chest. Her angel power pulsed, lighting the alley with its glow, and the demon screamed at an unholy pitch that no human would hear. However, the man cried out as well—how could he not? The demon was being ripped from his very soul, cleaving him at the DNA level, for that was the nature of this foul infection. The winter fae were behind this resurgence of demons in Seattle, as she had suspected all along—but now the House of Smoke had proof that vampires were preying on humans with their demon-infected bite. But all thoughts of the mechanisms and conspiracies were lost as the demon gave way under her blade. The pulse of pleasure that ran through her with that liberation vibrated her body, and she couldn't help but gasp and shudder with it, tipping her head back and reveling in the pure joy. This was no lust of the body—this was a pure and righteous pleasure! She had never felt the carnal pleasures—not so much as a kiss, as her Virtue of Chastity was very much intact—but she could imagine no earthly pleasure could approach the ecstasy of a good demon kill.

As it swept through her—a wave that left her trembling and yet on fire—the human slumped to the ground. The demon was vanquished, but his tarry black essence still dripped from her blade. She swept it with her hand, wiping the clear, heaven-wrought material clean once more, then sheathed it. The man lived, which surged joy through her heart. She knelt down and took the man's weathered cheeks in her hands. He was older and fragile and wracked by his time of living in desperation. She would never understand why humans found no way to care for the most vulnerable among them—they had so many gifts bestowed! But she supposed if the humans created a heaven on earth, then she might never experience the righteous pleasure of bestowing her kiss upon those in need.

She pressed her mouth to the man's—open and wide to breathe *life* into him—and she blessed him with all the love she possessed. She was only half angel, so her kiss could never have the power of a True Angel, like Markos or the other Protector Class Seraphim who shepherded angelings in the Chastity Faction. Erelah's mother had been human, and so her human side would always hold her back from perfection. Not that humans weren't a glory and a beauty and a sign of God's presence in the world— they absolutely were, and Erelah loved every last one, as any angel would. But God gifted humans with free will, and that meant struggle. And lo, how Erelah *struggled.* Sometimes, she thought she must secretly be more human than most angelings. But at least in this moment—this bestowing of a life kiss on a human she had just saved from a demon—she was the most purely *angel* she would ever be.

And the pleasure of that was an ecstasy that left her panting, her body humming and her mind buzzing.

Erelah climbed to standing, bringing the man with her, still engaged in the life kiss. She was not eager to break it, and neither was he, judging by the small moans coming from his throat. But finally, she was forced to release him. There was only so much she could give in a single kiss without resting, but more importantly, there was only so much the man's heart could take before crashing from the sheer joy of it. And this one was elderly and frail to begin with.

The man stumbled back when she released him. She would have swooped in to catch him, but he found his footing. She tipped her head back, eyes closed, relishing the last wave of ecstasy as it left her body. Her wings flexed, soaking it in, then she was forced to open her eyes as the scuffing sound of shoes pattered in front of her. The man had stumbled back, but then frozen, gaping at her, no doubt shocked by her angelic appearance in a dingy alleyway in Seattle.

"Peace be with you." She gestured to him with open hands. She understood being stunned after a life kiss—humans usually needed a little greeting or some encouragement to be on their way. He took her blessing and stumbled down the alley.

She let out a long, satisfied sigh as she watched him go. Demon-slaying was by far the best part of any day, and it couldn't happen enough for her tastes. It was righteous—there was no question of that—but she wondered as she peered after the man if perhaps she was becoming too fond of its pleasures. Could a righteous lust contain the hidden potential for a carnal one? She would always put her duty first, but what if her duty tempted her to a Sin which would destroy her? That must be the human inside her whispering temptation, not the angel…

Leksander's soft exhale next to her made her jolt.

She'd nearly forgotten his presence.

But thoughts of duty reminded her of the true reason she brought him on her demon hunts. She surely could rid the city of demons faster and better than when encumbered by the dragon prince, but Leksander needed her to cajole and convince and browbeat him into performing his own duty. His reluctance was an irritant on so many levels —she was forbidden by her duty from the carnal pleasures of her human side, but Leksander's duty virtually *required* that he indulge in them. And yet, one would think he had taken a Chastity vow himself with how he shirked away from it!

The two were such a strange pairing. It was not the first time she had thought this. But she was Markos's liaison to the House of Smoke, a duty she fell into by happenstance but which had taken on epic, world-ending levels of importance as of late. She had helped the first two princes with their mates and dragonlings—she would not fail in securing this last, and final, mating for the House of Smoke.

"If the bars are not to your liking," she said, turning to face Leksander and crossing her arms over her chest. "I believe there is an app which can serve the same purpose. It has presumably more discretion if that is your concern—"

"That's not my concern." There was a torment on his face which she didn't understand.

Erelah pursed her lips. Perhaps she was simply not trying hard enough to plumb the depths of the prince's troubled mind. It seemed straight-forward enough to her, but then many human-centric things seemed like they should be straightforward and yet weren't. She had not been raised among humans—few angelings were, and then only those in shadow. Leksander hadn't exactly grown up in the human world either, but dragons were not so different from the humans with which they mated. The angel dominions were an entirely different realm, with different rules and expectations and less… *complexity.* Or perhaps humans and dragons just seemed complex because they were a mystery to her. A delightful mystery, but a mystery nonetheless.

And yet, it was her mission to solve it. Markos made that much *very* clear. "What is your concern?" she asked, as gently as she knew how. "I wish to understand it."

The torment of unknown source continued on his face. "I just would like…" He looked away from her to the crumbling alleyway wall.

She looked to it as well, but there was nothing there she could see.

He gently tapped his fist against the wall and bit his lip. She knew him well enough, all these years, to know he was frustrated and choosing the appropriate words.

She waited.

He finally looked back to her. "The treaty requires a woman to fall in True Love with me. It's not *required* that I love her, but I honestly don't know how I would win someone's heart if I didn't."

Erelah frowned. "Human women fall in love with your kind all the time. I've seen it happen. It happens as well with the Seraphim. It is how so many of them Fall."

"You mean, they mate with humans." Leksander sighed like he was frustrated again.

"Yes." Was that not what she just said?

"Erelah, I'm going to spend the rest of my days with this woman," Leksander complained. "I'm going to have a child with her. I *want* to love her."

Erelah opened her mouth to scold him—what they *want* is not nearly as important as fulfilling their *duties*, and *lo* the duties he had were no less than world-shattering—but she stopped. And closed her mouth again. Because that argument had been had between them more times than she could count. She needed a *new* strategy. A new understanding of this dragon prince who was also her friend. Because this endless argument was getting her nowhere.

She wouldn't dishonor Leksander by assuming duty wasn't important to him—she knew him too well for that, and besides, he had proven it on more occasions than she could number. But this *wanting*... it was vexing him, and thus it was a problem to be solved. Perhaps it was similar to her desire for demon-slaying—that act slaked a need deep inside her and kept her on the righteous path with her vow of Chastity. Humans tempted her far less when she was fresh off a demon kill. Demon-slaying was something she *wanted* that helped her to fulfill her *duty*.

Aha. It felt as if a light went on in her mind.

Leksander was watching her curiously but without speaking. She tended to get lost in her own thoughts at times, and Leksander's practice of the Virtue of Patience with her was exemplary. It made him a very worthy friend.

She stepped up to him, gently took him by the shoulders with both hands, and peered intently into his eyes. He appeared surprised that she would take such liberties, but she needed him to see she took this matter with the utmost gravity.

"Have you ever loved someone, Leksander?" she asked.

He jolted in her grip, so she let him go. Perhaps it was too shocking a question.

But he answered it, very quietly. "Yes."

She nodded, encouraging him. "Is this person still alive?" Her dragon prince had lived for five hundred years —he was at the end of his lifespan, which would only be extended if he successfully mated and produced a drag-onling. Not just the life of the treaty hung in the balance, which made it personally important to Erelah. Leksander had been her friend and steadfast ally since her first foray out of Markos's Dominion when she came of age. Other than the angeling cohort she trained with as a child, he was her oldest friend. She did not want to see him die, not for many, many years to come.

Leksander was having trouble with her question. Maybe he didn't know the answer? If he had lost track of this human he loved...

"Yes, she's still alive," he said, finally.

She frowned. All of this would be much easier if this woman were dead. Or had simply fallen in love with him in the first place. "She must not be very intelligent."

A smile broke out on his face, the sweet kind that his family tended to have. The dragons of the House of Smoke were all tender of heart—this she knew from her years of personal experience with them, and most recently, with all the troubles with mating.

"What makes you say that?" he asked, the smile playing on his face.

"If she were smart," Erelah said, "she would have fallen in love with you when she first met you."

Leksander burst out laughing, so she scowled. She was being serious, and moreover, this was serious business. Given the number of human women that fell in love with the dragon princes on a regular basis, there must be some-thing wrong with the one who had not. Which was unfor-tunate because the treaty required True Love of

Leksander's mate. This presented a problem, one she wasn't sure how to approach.

She waited until his laughter settled to a merry look in his eyes. "Do you *still* love this woman?" she asked. Because if so, the problem was even more dire. And she could see why all her efforts to engage Leksander in a hunt for the perfect mate had been as productive as asking a demon to voluntarily step into the light. Would she need the equivalent of an angel dagger to the chest to convince Leksander to move on?

All humor fled the dragon prince's face. His seriousness was now equal to the moment, but her concern was doubled. Because this *wanting* of his might *not* be in service of his duty.

"What about you, Erelah?" he asked, voice suddenly hushed as if they were discussing secrets. "Have you ever loved someone?"

"I love all humans." But this was irritating—he was changing the subject.

"Someone in particular," he pressed, eyes alight. "Anyone at all? Even your parents?"

She let out a tight sigh, but if this discussion was what he desired… perhaps it would lead him to release this prior love and embracing his duty.

"I didn't know my mother long enough to remember her." Erelah had the faintest memory of a woman with long, blonde hair like her own, but she couldn't be sure it wasn't a fantasy. All angelings spoke of their mothers with reverence, but Erelah never understood how they could *know them*—angelings were all taken away to a Dominion of the Light at nearly the moment of their births. "I imagine that I must have loved my mother. I've seen your dragonling princes at the moments of their births—young Larik and little Thorn. They seemed to gaze up at their mothers with love, and certainly, their mothers held great and obvious love for them. I must have been the same, perhaps even more so—after all, my mother is human, and I am half angel. I could not help but love her."

But this answer was not satisfying Leksander—she could tell by the wrinkling of his brow and the pinched-together state of his ice-blue eyes. "I'm sorry, Erelah. I didn't realize…"

"Sorry for what?" She could see nothing to be sorry for. Dragons seriously confused her sometimes.

"I didn't know that you never knew your mother." He looked very troubled by this.

So she tried to put him at ease. "All angelings are taken from their mothers at birth. This is for the best."

"How can you say that?" His troubled expression grew darker.

"Because I'm immortal? Because she is already long dead?" This seemed obvious to her, but she tried to walk it back and see how to explain it better. "It is a Fall from grace when a Seraphim loses himself in love with a human female. It's understandable—all of angelkind feels that tug, that desire for communion with the wonder of God's creation—but it's also a tragedy. For that child can never live with humanity—they are too much angel. And that angeling will never be one with the Seraphim—they have too much human within them. They are forever stuck between worlds."

"I know." Leksander's eyes held a light that was true Kindness. Erelah could feel the Virtue hum inside him. "I've always thought that angelings had it hardest of all the creatures, like dragons, who are mixed. It's difficult enough to always be part human and part *something else*. But in your case…" He reached out to gently tuck back a stray wisp of her hair that was floating beside her. "That *something else* is entirely different." He drew back his hand and frowned. "You may not have known your mother, but surely you must love your father."

She frowned. Whereas her human mother was obviously without fault in Erelah's birth, the same could not be said for her father. "My father is shadow now. It is part of the Fall. I do not love things which exist in darkness." How did this conversation get so far off track?

Leksander drew back at the harshness in her tone. "But he's an angel, right?"

"An angel of darkness." Why were they discussing her shame? It was not relevant and surely wouldn't help Leksander find his mate, which was the business at hand. Leksander was scowling darkly now, so she gripped his shoulder with one hand to bring him back to focus. "None of that matters. What matters is finding you a mate. If we find one you can love, then all the better. But your duty is clear, Leksander, and all depends on you not wavering from it. Lust and love and whatever your personal feelings might be… they cannot interfere. I want to help you—you are my most steadfast of friends—but you seem determined to skirt this duty, and I do not understand why."

Leksander's face was twisted in turmoil again, but he just stepped back from her touch. "I know you don't." He nodded as if affirming something to himself. "I just have to… figure this out." He held her gaze intently for a moment. "By myself."

Then he shifted into his lustrous silver dragon form and lifted from the alleyway.

She watched him go and felt her failure like a strike against her heart. She had *tried* to understand him, and yet he was winging away upset and no closer to the goal.

At times, she felt her ineptness to this task as if it were bred into her at the moment of her birth. She didn't know her father any more than her mother, but she imagined he must be the most incompetent of angels that ever drew holy breath. For all her fumbling and bumbling must have come from *somewhere.* And that thought haunted her, like a demon that presaged her own Fall to come. Her ardent pursuit of the demons that riddled Seattle was not merely for the pleasure or even the righteousness, but for the *certainty* that with each one slain, she was still on the path of the Light. But tonight, with Leksander flying off on his own, even demon-hunting had lost its allure. She should return to her Dominion and contemplate where she had gone wrong. And then try once more in assisting her friend. Leksander may wish to tackle this alone, but she would be ready at arms the instant he needed her.

With a heavy heart, she spread her wings and rose from the alley.

Chapter Two

Leksander dashed through the halls of the keep.

He was late. If there was any indication of the turmoil in his life, that had to be it. He *loathed* being late. For anything, really, but for an official function of the House of Smoke? The embarrassment was like dragonfire he'd swallowed that was now consuming him from the inside out.

He arrived at the throne room but hesitated at the door. He could hear the rustlings of the dragons gathered inside. Now that they had returned to the keep outside Seattle, the entire House would be turned out for the official presentation of gifts from around the immortal world. Rosalyn and Leonidas had earned this celebration of their son, Thorn, Leksander's newest nephew… and they deserved better than to have him rush in halfway through the ceremonies. But there was only one door in, and he couldn't travel back in time, so…

He pulled open the doors and marched in with as much dignity as he could manage.

He gathered stares, which he ignored. Besides being late, he had to look like hell. He'd been exhaustively hunting demons with Erelah since they returned three days ago, keeping all hours of the night and day with that. And even when he was in his lair, his sleep was fitful. He knew the circles under his eyes were just getting darker, even as he avoided looking in the mirror. Those all-day runs with Erelah were his last-ditch attempt to discern her heart. Did she love him, in her own angeling way? If not, *could* she love him? Had she ever loved *anyone* in her entire, nearly one-hundred-year existence in the mortal and immortal realms?

Last night, the answers were *no* on all counts. And his heart had been banished to the cellar of his soul because of it.

After a long, torturous march, he finally reached the front. Leonidas and Rosalyn sat on their receiving thrones. Leonidas had baby Thorn cradled in one arm, fast asleep —rumor was that he rarely relinquished the child to anyone—while Rosalyn peered on with a smile in her eyes. Leksander gave the shortest bow in the history of House functions then slunk off to the side to stand next to Cinaed and his beloved, Rachel. She didn't yet bear Cinaed's mark, at least as far as Leksander could taste with his fae senses, but rumor held that their mating was imminent. He didn't know what the man was waiting for—finding a mate was something every dragon strove for—but now that little Thorn had been successfully born, Cinaed might settle his own affairs and start his own family.

Leksander gave him a nod and silently wished him well in that—the entire House knew that *Leksander's* mating would be nothing so simple. If he managed it at all.

There were no guests present, *thank magic.* At least he hadn't brought *that* embarrassment on his House. On top of the shame of being late, everyone had to know he'd not truly begun the search for a mate yet, something upon which everyone depended. The House of Smoke was built on the treaty. The royals of the House were duty-bound to preserve it. In this, Erelah was exceedingly correct.

Even if she was blind to his feelings for her. Feelings which he needed to bury once and for all… for the good of everyone. Even if it tore into him, leaving him hollow like nothing he'd ever—

An elbow stabbed into his side and jerked him out of his thoughts.

He scowled at Cinaed. *"What?"* he hissed.

Cinaed's eyes were wide with some hint he was trying to throw, but he didn't speak, just jutted out his chin toward the thrones.

Rosalyn was beckoning him.

Oh, for magic's sake. Leksander sucked in a breath and strode over to the dais and bowed in front of it. "My apologies for my tardiness, my lady. My brother." He nodded to Leonidas who just shrugged and only had eyes for his son. Leksander's gaze swung back to Rosalyn. "I'm sorry, Rosalyn—"

"Come here, you big dork," she said in a quiet voice, not meant for the hall. She gestured him closer to her throne.

He climbed the two steps to stand next to her, turning to face the restless crowd of dragons. He didn't know what they were waiting for—probably some arrogant angel like Markos to make his appearance and present his gifts. Seeing that oversized, nearly-naked paragon of angel righteousness was that last thing Leksander needed right now. Erelah may not profess to love anyone—not even her own parents—but the way she looked at Markos set Leksander's blood to boiling. If sex between angels and angelings weren't forbidden, he was sure she would take a ride on his angelic cock.

"Earth to Leksander," Rosalyn hush-whispered next to him.

He jolted back to awareness again. He needed some sleep. "I'm sorry, I just…" He shook his head. There were really no excuses.

"Leksander, you look beat." Rosalyn frowned.

"Sleep is… *elusive* at the moment, princess." As if the words summoned a yawn, he pressed the back of his hand to his mouth to stifle one.

She nodded sagely. "It would be worth it if you were up all night with Erelah. *Not* hunting demons, I mean."

"Unfortunately, no." Although his hand had gotten the usual workout, stroking away his frustrations to fantasies of Erelah *sans* those barely-there wisps of angeling clothing. He gave up seeking relief with other women decades ago —it was just too pathetic, if not downright embarrassing when he called out Erelah's name mid-climax. Better to get off in his own lair, safely ensconced in his dreams… which were the only places where Erelah professed an affection for him, either lust or love.

Shame burned through him with how pathetic the state of his love life had been, and the long number of years it had been that way.

Rosalyn was scowling at him. "You promised me that you'd tell her."

"I made no such promise." His words were a little too sharp—Leonidas looked up from his baby-gazing.

"Don't try it, bro," Leonidas warned. "Just give Rosalyn whatever she wants. We'll all be happier for it."

"Not *all* of us." But Leksander's bitterness was pointed at the wrong woman. "I'm sorry, Rosalyn. None of this is your fault. *Magic knows* the two of you have done far more for the House of Smoke than I've ever managed."

Rosalyn wasn't done, however. "Just tell her, Leksander!

I swear to God, it won't kill you. However, I might steal Erelah's blade and threaten your neck if you don't get busy! It's not like you've got time to spare."

Truth. It was all truth. But that didn't change one bit about the reality of the situation. "I spoke with her last night," Leksander said, his stomach tightening with the hopeful look in Rosalyn's eyes. "Nothing happened. And that's precisely my point. Nothing is *going* to happen. She doesn't love me, and what's more, I'm certain she's never loved anyone."

"No one?" Rosalyn's face held pity, and Leksander supposed that was the right response, but to him, all it meant was hopelessness.

"No one. Not even her parents."

Rosalyn drew back in her chair like she didn't believe him.

Leksander waved away her concern. Or perhaps disbelief. "It's an angel thing. Which is exactly the problem. She's *not* human. She's not even a witch like you, or a shifter, or anything else from the mortal realm. She's *unearthly,* Rosalyn. And I'm afraid that loving someone like me isn't in the realm of possibilities for someone like her. That's just... something I have to finally face, now that we're..." He gestured vaguely to baby Thorn. "...in the situation we're in."

Even Leonidas's face held an ocean of sympathy now. "I'm sorry, my brother."

Leksander sucked in a breath. "Yes, well... me too. But there's nothing to be done about it. I'll start looking elsewhere for a mate. Soon." At the skepticism in his brother's eyes, he quickly added, "Tomorrow. All right? Tomorrow is the day."

Rosalyn was scowling again. "Let me talk to her."

"No!" It came out loud and furious, like a suddenly

uncorked volcano. Leonidas's eyes flew wide, and Rosalyn drew further back. Even Leksander felt the shock of it. Every dragon in the House turned to stare, dropping their banter to whispers. Leonidas's shock turned into a glare, and he looked like he might throw down for a fight if he weren't holding his infant son.

"I'm sorry," Leksander rushed out. "I'm on edge and…" *Heartbroken.* He swallowed. He didn't want to give it voice for fear that more than a shouted word or two would come bellowing out of his mouth. "I'm sorry," he said again. "Rosalyn, my lady," he pleaded, "if there's no chance of her returning my love, much less having the kind of True Love the treaty requires, *please* spare me the horror of her knowing my feelings in this. I'm not just trying to avoid a stomping of my heart. I know her too well. She would try some foolish exercise or worse…" He pressed his lips together and leaned away as if fearing to even think about it. Because what would Erelah do? He *did* know her —strong and brash and powerful. Committed to giving everything to protect humanity. If she thought for one moment *she* was the one standing in the way of the treaty being renewed—that a love-sick dragon prince couldn't get over his attachment to her—he shuddered to think what she might do. Angelings were longer-lived and harder to kill than dragons, but he wouldn't put it past her to go out in some blaze of glory somehow justified by the complicated code of ethics the angel realm seemed to employ. It was mysterious to him, but one thing was clear—the angels and their begotten, the angelings, were nothing if not radically committed to their righteousness.

"She would give *anything* to protect the treaty," he whispered. "I don't want her to do something rash."

Rosalyn's eyes went wide, but she had to know. Erelah's blade saved her and baby Thorn. She had to see the zeal that gripped Erelah. "I won't say anything," Rosalyn said quietly.

The House had gone back to whispering amongst themselves, although subdued. As if Leksander's outburst had put a pall over them, reminding them that the business of the treaty was as yet unfulfilled.

"Thank you," Leksander said with true gratitude.

"However, I still think *you* should." She went back to frowning.

Leksander just rolled his eyes and shook his head. The time for that was long past. In this, Erelah was correct—he needed to buckle down and get to the business of seducing a woman to carry his dragonling. If he were lucky, maybe he would even grow fond of her. It was possible, he supposed. The main problem would be that he hadn't seduced a woman in decades—not since he realized that his fascination with a certain beautiful angeling had morphed into something much stronger and more persistent and, ultimately, more destructive than simple lust.

And all these years, he kept hoping, kept wishing, that she would finally find her way to loving him. But he should have known—if it was possible for an angeling to love a dragon, it would have happened years ago. If Erelah could be a woman first and an angel second—at least with him— she would have noticed the time and slavish attention he'd given her for decades. But it had become painfully obvious to everyone—including him—that it would not happen.

He was a fool for ever thinking otherwise.

From the first moment they met, his runes had always danced in her presence—not because there was any magic attraction between them, but because his blood contained summer fae magic, and the fae and angels were natural enemies. It would be worse if his ancestor was winter fae instead of summer... then again, a winter fae would never care enough to fall in love with a dragon. Nor protect humanity with her magic. And *any* fae was far more likely to fall in love with a dragon than an angeling ever would be.

Now that the treaty depended solely on him, he couldn't afford to indulge the fantasy any longer.

A sudden hush fell over the throne room and drew his attention. The far door—the one he'd come through—opened of its own accord, some magic in play. The wards were down, and Leksander hadn't kept up with the schedule of visitors, but he didn't have to wait long to see who was next up in the queue.

The Queen of the Summer Fae strolled through the open doorway, hips swaying and a smile playing on her lips. The queen's beauty rivaled that of any angeling—the fae and the fallen had more in common than they might wish to think. They were rivals precisely because of their immortal beauty and insanely powerful magic. Just a few drops of fae blood, diluted by ten generations, still powered Leksander to magic that was greater than any other mortal species. Yet the way the queen strutted down the center of the long throne room, her ethereally silver dress wrapped tightly around her curves, her waves of silver-white hair floating in a long train behind her, was far more seductive than a show of power. Or much like a head of state coming to pay respects to the new prince of the House of Smoke. The way her eyes roamed the bodies of the male dragons, and even a few of their mates, was astonishing in its frankness.

Leksander wracked his memory for when the queen had visited the first time, on the advent of little Larik's birth. She seemed much more… *reserved*… then. She had bestowed the bronze dragon totem which ended up saving Thorn's life—was this new attitude part of that?

Leksander's brain was too tired to sort it out, but the way Leonidas rose from his throne and handed his son off to his mate put Leksander's teeth on edge. He stepped down from the dais with Leonidas, standing protectively in front of the mother and child, as the fae queen arrived at the front.

Her smile for Leonidas and Leksander was no less lusty than the gazes she swept over every other dragon. With a wave of her hand, she conjured an enormous butterfly that seemed made of light—a bluish magical light. It hovered over her palm, and as the queen lifted her hand, it fluttered to Leonidas, hovering in front of his face.

"Well, go on," the queen said with a smile. "Take it. I promise you, it won't bite."

Leonidas gave her a pinched look but raised his hand, palm up. The magical butterfly, as big as Leonidas's head, alighted on his hand and instantly transformed into a tiny crystalline version of the same.

"Another totem?" Leonidas asked.

"The first one worked splendidly." She smiled wider. "So I hear. This one will watch over the child. A protection against all ailments in the future. With any luck, it will not be necessary to use it."

Leonidas nodded, and his shoulders seemed to relax. "The House of Smoke is tremendously grateful for your gift. You have my personal gratitude for helping save both my son and my mate as well."

At the mention of Rosalyn, she rose from her throne, baby Thorn in her arms. She stepped forward, peering over Leonidas's shoulder. "We haven't met," she said to the queen, "but you should know that your magic lives on in both my son and me."

"Yes, dear, I know." The queen's smile turned into a smirk. "I sensed you the moment I was in the keep." She swept her gaze over the entire royal family. "Fae magic is hard to miss."

Leksander's runes were certainly dancing up and down his body in response to the queen's powerful magic so nearby.

"Well, thank you," Rosalyn added. "I doubt there's anything we can do to repay you, but if there is, please let us know."

The queen's nearly colorless blue eyes glittered, and her smirk grew in a hungry way. Leksander shot a glance at Leonidas—his brother's entire body had stiffened.

"You know what I want, Leonidas," the queen purred.

Rosalyn frowned and looked to him, but it wasn't until Leonidas gave her an embarrassed shake of the head—as if she shouldn't ask him, not now in front of everyone— that Leksander finally remembered what this was about. And the debt the queen was here to collect.

Leonidas had warned them about the bargain he had struck—the queen forced Zephan, Prince of the Winter Court, to release Rosalyn in exchange for unspecified favors of a sexual nature for the queen. Not with Leonidas, but rather with some random dragon from the House of Smoke. Or dragons, plural. Apparently, the queen had a taste for them like her mother before her—where it had been ten generations for the House of Smoke since the treaty was formed, Queen Nyssa was the direct descendent of the original fae queen who fell in love with a dragon and spawned the entire House of Smoke lineage.

Leonidas gave a slow nod to the queen. "The House of Smoke will honor its debt to you, Nyssa. But only volunteers. And I expect them to return—*alive*—from your bedchambers."

A rustle of sucked-in breaths flitted across the throne room.

Leksander grimaced. *Alive?* He had assumed that sleeping with a fae would be a dangerous business, but was this even worse than he thought? It was difficult to kill a dragon… unless you were *fae*. It wasn't hard to imagine Nyssa accidentally smiting her lover in the throes of her passion.

Nyssa barely tipped her head in acknowledgment to Leonidas's condition before turning to saunter slowly past the standing legion of dragon warriors in attendance. To their credit, they were mostly unflinching under her long, lascivious looks up and down their bodies, checking them out in the most obvious way.

Leksander gritted his teeth. The woman was certainly taking her time. She made the entire circuit, down to the door and back. Finally, she stopped next to Cinaed. He went rigid before her, eyes wide. His love, Rachel, stood next to him.

"Oh, hell no—" she said, but Cinaed cut her off with a wave of his hand.

He stood stoically under the queen's gaze, but Nyssa just smirked and moved to the dragon standing next to him. It was Dirk, a youngish dragon not long in the House. Leksander scoured his memories, but he couldn't recall the young dragon having yet taken a mate.

He stood straight under the queen's examination.

Finally, she breathed out in a whisper full of promise, "This one." Then she reached out a single finger to stroke Dirk's cheek.

His eyes fell shut, and his mouth fell open. His gasp was unmistakably sexual, plus the instant erection that strained against his formalwear pants, loose and draped as befit the custom for the House's royal ceremonies. Then he dropped to his knees, the full effect of whatever Nyssa was doing apparently ramping up.

Still touching his face, the queen seemed equally affected, her voice ragged as she whispered, "Oh yes." Then she withdrew her hand, and Dirk reeled back, gasping.

But it definitely wasn't in pain.

And that was just with a single touch. *Holy fuck.*

The effect on the room was instant—the tension was gone, and Leksander imagined every unmated dragon was now highly interested in finding out just exactly what Dirk had experienced... and how they could be next in Nyssa's bed.

The fae queen bid Dirk to rise with a flutter of her fingers. Leksander had never seen a man move so fast to obey. He was on his feet and by her side in a flash.

Nyssa turned to face the front dais. "This one will do. For now," she said to Leonidas. Then, without waiting for a response or turning to Dirk, she reached back, clasped his arm, then twisted and disappeared in a flash of light.

A release of held breaths sighed throughout the room.

"Don't know if we'll be seeing him anytime soon," Leonidas said with a chuckle, returning to sit on his receiving throne. Rosalyn took her seat as well.

Leksander no longer worried about Dirk's fate—the man he might not even *want* to return. Which was fine— the affairs of the fae were the least of his concerns at the moment.

Rosalyn's wide-eyed look had given way to whispering something to her mate. Leonidas gave her a curious look, arched an eyebrow, then lifted his chin to Leksander to have him draw near. The throne room had descended into a frenzy of whispered conversations anyway, and they had time before whoever was slated to visit next. Leksander stepped over to Leonidas's throne—baby Thorn was once again tucked in the crook of his arm.

"Yes?" Leksander asked.

Leonidas was fighting a smirk. "When Nyssa returns, perhaps you should go next."

"*What?*" Was his brother serious? Leksander shot a look to Rosalyn—she was leaning over the edge of her throne to nod encouragingly. "For the love of magic…" Did they just *forget* he had an urgent need to find a mate?

Leonidas cocked an eyebrow. "Seducing the summer queen would be about as difficult as breathing."

"Only a lot more dangerous." Leksander scowled. "Besides, I've another urgent matter to attend to. Even if I'm loathe to do it."

"Just hear me out," Leonidas said, holding up his baby-free hand. "It's not as if a fae queen has never fallen in love with a dragon before."

Leksander drew back. His brother truly had gone mad.

"*And,*" Leonidas continued, "think of it, my brother. If you could win the queen's heart, your mating would be… fantastically powerful. It would renew the treaty in a way that was previously unthinkable. And *unbreakable.* The strength of the fae blood in your dragonling alone… I know your heart remains with Erelah, but if mating is not possible for you two, the strategic merits of this are almost impossible to calculate."

Leksander scowled more and more with each word. His heart was bruised and battered… *but this?* Mating with a fae queen? "It matters not if she's Queen of the Summer Court. Her love would have to be True to renew the treaty. And I just don't think…" Leksander shook his head. It was madness.

Leonidas nodded. "I'll admit it's far-fetched. But what's the worst that could happen, my brother? You haven't been in a woman's bed for… how long? Decades now?"

Leksander just growled at him.

Leonidas held up his hand for peace again. "I'm just saying. Some mind-blowing sex with the fae queen might be just what you need to *move on* from a certain angeling's grip on your heart. Then, if sex is all the queen desires, you'll be ready to get to the business of seducing a woman to be your mate. Think about it, my brother. That's all I'm saying."

"And don't take too long about it," Rosalyn added.

They both gave her a somewhat startled look. But she just rose from her throne and planted her hands on her hips. "You *deserve* someone who loves you, Leksander," she said, fiercely staring up at him. "Either that angeling of yours figures it out, or you get together with the fae queen, or *something.* But this business of waiting around to have your heart stomped on? *No.*" She dashed a look to Leonidas, and the love in her eyes sprang a stab of jealousy through Leksander's heart. He couldn't help but want Erelah to look at him that way. The fact that she never would... Rosalyn turned back to face him. She had tears in her eyes. "You can't just *wait* for love, Leksander. You have to *fight* for it."

He nodded quickly—because what argument could he have against that? When he'd watched the two of them risk everything for their love, he knew she was speaking the truth. And that was precisely the kind of love he was willing to give... and had been all along. He just needed to find someone willing—and able—to return it.

He glanced at his brother. "You're a lucky man, Leonidas."

"I know that every damn minute of the day," he said solemnly.

Leksander faced Rosalyn again. "Okay. If the queen returns, I'll see what interest she might have in a dragon prince. And if she doesn't..." He swallowed. "I'll start my search on the morrow. I promise you, Rosalyn. I will give this my full devotion."

She gave a short nod of approval.

As much as he meant that promise, it still filled him with dread. The open wound in his heart—the one he had carried for decades—needed some kind of solace to close it before he could even begin to make good on his words. Maybe his brother was right. Maybe some knee-buckling sex with an exotic fae queen would be just the searing he needed to cauterize that wound. So he could move on.

One way or another, he had to make this work.

Chapter Three

Erelah's warrior cry shook the crystal walls around her.

She dove from the pinnacle of the training room, wings tucked back, blade held out, and rushed at the phantom hovering along the floor. Her landing stuck with a crackling that rippled through the crystalline structure of the room. She pinned the phantom while simultaneously plunging her blade into its body. The thing evaporated into mist. There was no joy, no surge of demon-killing pleasure, just the cool satisfaction of sharpening her skills.

For this phantom was not a true demon, just a training dummy, conjured of magic and righteous intent. The true demons were still haunting Seattle, but she couldn't bring herself to hunt alone, without Leksander. Her failure to understand him, much less help him in his duty, was eating away at her and pitching her into a bleakness of mind that made it impossible to think. And she *needed* to think. There had to be some way to help him that she was missing, but her unsettled state made it almost impossible to figure out.

Hence, the hours in the training room.

Normally, the other angelings would use the room as well, but her beleaguered cries and hours of relentless "kills" had driven off everyone. The room was constructed of the same massive, translucent crystal beams that comprised all of Markos's Dominion, and like all angel realms, it existed in a magical space outside the normal, mortal world. Only angels or angelings could travel here—or the fae, if they had a death wish about them. Erelah had brought Leksander to visit a few times, and the wonder on his face had made her smile. It was her home, a refuge from a mortal realm that did not understand her kind, but he was suitably awed by the endless shimmering corridors of the Dominion, each magic-crystal-encased cloister cell serving the angels and angelings who dwelt there. It was a palace of light and beauty, a stronghold for the Virtues they all strived for, and Leksander seemed to delight in it as much as she did.

Now she was not only alone without his company—rebuked by him in her failure to help—but she'd driven off her fellow angelings as well with her ill-temper. Patience was the Virtue she struggled with most, and even the exertion of the training room couldn't wholly bring it within her grasp.

Her body hummed with the power stoked by her frustration, and she let loose with another cry, arms held high, eyes closed, mouth wide…

When the echoes of her angelsong faded, a plain voice said, "No wonder you're alone."

She popped open her eyes and whirled, blade raised, to face the one mocking her.

It was just Tajael.

He was one of her cohort, the five angelings brought to Markos's Dominion at the same time as her, and he was her oldest friend. The other three—Sajit, Oriel, and Halo

—had either gone shadow, in the case of Sajit, or apprenticed out to other Dominions. Oriel was still in the Chastity faction, but under another Seraphim, Raeph. Halo had found the Patience faction more to her suiting. Erelah had seen none of them since that initial foray out into the mortal realm when they all came of age. Only Tajael remained with her, here in Markos's Dominion.

Beyond Leksander, he was her most trusted aid in all things.

"I'm not in the mood for mocking, Tajael," she said, sheathing her blade and giving him a small frown.

He gestured to the glistening walls around them. "All the training in the world cannot prepare you for the level of mocking of which I am capable." But his smile was gentle. Her friend was far more accomplished in the human social arts than she was, especially the Virtues of Charity and Kindness. He somehow knew how to say the right things at just the right moments to ease the burdens of humans, which was why Markos often sent him out on guardian angel duty. She, on the other hand, had never quite grasped the nuances of the human world as Tajael had. But then he nearly went shadow during his walkabout on earth, which lasted five years to Erelah's six months. It almost cost him his wings. Erelah quickly saw the folly of that, at least for her—she didn't have his skills—and she'd retreated to living in the Dominion once again. She understood that realm and the company of angels and angelings who expected nothing but the best from her. To some extent, she understood the dragon realm as well. Or perhaps, not as well as she thought, given her failure with Leksander.

Tajael's easy stroll had finally brought him to her side. His gentle frown worked its way into her chest, tightening it. "You're troubled," he said, like this pained him. "And here I am, bearing yet more bad news."

"What bad news?" She peered behind him, but he was alone. He wore the standard lightweight toga that mostly bared his chest but draped further to the floor—not tightly wrapped sparing clothes like she had on, so he wasn't here to train, either. Had something happened in the House of Smoke? Her stomach felt even more hollow than it did the day before when Leksander flew away.

"Markos knows you're here, of course." Tajael paused, seeming to hesitate to say more.

"He knows of my, uh, disagreement with the dragon prince?" She'd not mentioned anything to Markos—he expected results, not complaints—but apparently, her mere presence in the Dominion and not out on the streets of Seattle was cause for concern.

"A disagreement?" Tajael asked, eyebrows lifting.

Erelah's shoulders slumped. She should have said nothing. "The dragon prince is engaged in finding a mate." Not a falsehood, as far as she knew. Leksander *did* pledge to work on discerning his problem, namely his hesitation in seeking a mate to fulfill his duty. But she had no first-hand knowledge he was doing anything more than sleeping off their endless demon-hunting in his lair.

"Is he?" Tajael asked. "And yet you are here."

"Such a thing requires privacy at certain times." She pictured the sex that dragons seemed wired to seek constantly, and she couldn't help the squeamishness that accompanied that image. Such acts were required for the mating to occur—she knew that—but for her, those base passions led to the shadow side, and she couldn't quite break the connection in her head. It was perfectly right and necessary for humans and dragons to procreate. And God created that driving need for the act to ensure his creatures continued to populate the earth. But for angelkind, those urges were a constant danger that needed to be fought… lest they Fall. And then there would be no serving their higher purpose of protecting humanity, much less living out the Virtues.

She was lost in her own head again.

Tajael was peering at her, curiously. "It disturbs you. To encourage a mating." He liked to speak plainly. It was one of the things she respected about him.

She grimaced. "That's not holding me back from my duty. I would help Leksander in any way I could. But none of my encouragements or strategies seem to find purchase with him."

Tajael frowned. "But you are friends, are you not?"

"I believe so." Those words conjured the image of Leksander winging away from her, and that stab of pain went through her chest again like a needle-sharp angel blade. Were they still friends? She couldn't imagine a world in which that wasn't true, but this treaty business trumped everything else. Perhaps it would destroy their friendship on the way to saving humanity. She couldn't help feeling the loss of that even pre-emptively.

Tajael was stroking his chin, bare of any whiskers even though he never shaved. His angel side was strong, eliminating many of the things human men required. Like razors. "In my experience, humans may not always trust others with their affairs of the heart. But your friendship is long-standing. One would think he would trust your intent."

"I fear it's not my intent that's lacking," she said with a cringe. "But my understanding of human ways."

Tajael nodded in a knowing fashion. "They are beautiful and noble, but complicated. Even the ones who are mixed with immortal blood are nothing like angelkind."

"Yes," she breathed. "Thank you. I was beginning to think I had gone mad."

He smiled gently. "No more mad than anyone here." He gestured to the empty training hall, but she took him to mean all of Markos's Dominion. "Speaking of, I came to warn you. Markos is—" Tajael cut himself off as he felt the same tremor in the air that sent a shiver of delight up Erelah's back.

Markos strode into the training hall a second later, the air humming with the power of his Virtues. He was a True Angel, the thing that all of them—every angeling in his Dominion—wished to attain, but in reality, never could. That was not a discouragement, though, because even in the seeking to perfect themselves, they were paying homage to the perfection embodied by God in angels like Markos. The Seraphim took human form whenever they were in the presence of angelings or humans or any creature lower than the Seraphim themselves, but it was just a disguise—an affectation to ease the discomfort of other beings while in the presence of so much holiness. Their true form was much like the Archangels, or even the Aeons—a pure energy, spun of magic and God's grace, that could create the crystal palace around them with merely a thought. The Aeons never donned human form, and the Archangels only rarely did—and only when revealing themselves to humans. But the Seraphim's duties brought them closest to humanity, including their hybrid angeling children, and they appeared human most of the time. Not that anyone would mistake them for mortal creatures.

Markos strode with an unearthly ease—no hurry, but with great power—across the crystalline floor of the training room. His toga revealed the glory of his God-made form, both larger than any normal-sized human and impossibly beautiful.

Erelah couldn't help but be entranced in his presence. And terrified.

For Markos wouldn't seek her out unless he was holding her to some account.

"Erelah." Just her name in his booming angel voice was enough to make her quail, both with excitement and dread. "Your aid in delivering the young prince of the House of Smoke has been noted."

"*Oh,*" she breathed. "Yes. The princess of the House of Smoke was very brave. And my blade ran true." She struggled not to feel the burst of pride that came from Markos's notice. Humility was a Virtue she found easier than all the others, save her strongest in Chastity, but it was a plain fact that the young dragonling, Thorn, would not have survived without her help. And pride in rendering service to humanity was no Sin.

"Your Diligence in assisting the House of Smoke is a credit to you."

"It is my honor to serve," she gave the ritual reply, but she could hardly contain her joy under that praise. She dared to sneak a glance at Tajael, but inexplicably, he was frowning.

No matter. Clearly, Markos was pleased with her.

"Your service has been truly Virtuous." Markos's voice dropped in its intensity, gentling to a more human tone. "But Tajael will serve the House of Smoke now."

Erelah just blinked. She heard Markos's words, but she couldn't believe what they were saying. "I... I don't understand."

"Your love for the House of Smoke has always been strong," Markos said gently. "This is no mark against you, young angeling. But I fear your judgment is yet clouded in this critical phase of the renewal of the treaty."

"I... but... I prevented the demon from being born!

Just as you wished!" She felt hot and angry, and she knew that was wrong. So was talking back to a Seraphim. She knew all that, but she couldn't help herself. It was so *unfair.*

"I know, child," Markos said gently. Then he reached his large hand toward her head, and Erelah steeled herself for the blessing. Even so, she gasped when his palm lightly pressed her forehead and the burst of angel power—of *life* itself—surged into her. It lifted her up and calmed the Sin of anger, pure wrath, that was boiling inside her. She'd only been blessed twice before—once just before voyaging out of the Dominion for the first time, and once again when she returned, Virtue intact, ready to take on the burden and joy of serving humanity. This one felt both a reward for a service well-rendered and a punishing destruction of her urgent need to protest against this injustice.

After Markos removed his hand and the blessing ceased, she still felt the unfairness of being yanked from her service to the House of Smoke before she could see her mission through. But that feeling didn't burn through her with the same dangerous and urgent need.

Markos nodded in approval at her more calm demeanor. "Tajael will go to them. He will explain and offer his assistance in any way. They will be well cared for, Erelah." Then he turned to Tajael. "Let them know they may call upon me. I will suffer no interference from the fae in this crucial matter. And give them this." Markos held out his palm. A beaming cube of light appeared hovering over it. *A blessing.* The cube floated out of his hand and into Tajael's waiting palm.

"I live to serve," Tajael said, the ritual words signaling his acceptance of the blessing and the mission.

The Sins of Envy and Wrath surged again in Erelah's chest, but her body still hummed with Markos's blessing, and she could contain them. Without another word, Markos turned and strode with slow, powerful steps from the training room.

Neither Tajael nor Erelah spoke until he was gone. Erelah, mostly because she had no words that weren't bitter or angry, despite the blessing trying to tamp those down within her human side.

Tajael finally broke the silence. "I will, of course, need your advice in this matter." A small smile was on his face.

She dashed a look to him. "But Markos said—"

Tajael arched his eyebrows. "Markos said this matter was crucial. And no one could question that—all of humanity is at stake. Which means I must draw on every available resource. And as far as I know, you are the angeling most versed in the ways of the House of Smoke." His smile grew. "And Markos said absolutely nothing forbidding you from accompanying me."

A surge of joy washed through her. "Tajael… if cleverness were a Virtue, God would lift you to Seraphim on the spot."

He chuckled. "I'm rather certain cleverness is more Sin than Virtue. But I'll concede that my plan has an almost human level of genius."

Erelah grinned wide then impulsively threw her arms around Tajael and hugged him hard. The angel essence within them both surged in protest—given they were two angelings of the Chastity faction, neither one of them could tolerate physical contact with any of angelkind for long. Erelah dutifully released him and stepped back, but the grin remained.

"You are a true friend," she said.

"And you are truly a badass for standing up to Markos." But his laughter was light under the teasing. "Let us get to our mission, shall we? There is no time to waste in the saving of all humanity." His smile was clear and bright, and all envy was banished from Erelah's heart.

With her friend's help, surely they would bring the House of Smoke through its final trial. How could they not, with Virtue on their side?

She gave Tajael a sharp nod, and together, they spread their wings and summoned the twisting of time and space that would bring them to the House of Smoke and the troubled prince therein who needed their help.

Chapter Four

THE QUEEN OF THE SUMMER FAE?

How much of a desperate fool was Leksander for even considering her bedchamber?

He'd excused himself from the ceremonial receiving of gifts for Leonidas and Rosalyn, explaining that he needed to formulate a plan for finding a mate. Then he retreated to the deep pool his brothers often used, but he seldom did. He'd spent an hour plunging to its depths buried the mountainside then soaring to the glass-enclosed heights. He'd beaten his wings and his talons against every dragon-proofed surface, including the rocky bottom of the pool, then he vented dragonfire until the entire cistern boiled. When he'd raged enough, he collapsed on the stone flagging at the edge of the pool, lying naked and staring up at the darkening twilight skies overhead.

He had never been one to brood like Lucian.

He'd never had Leonidas's gallows humor, born of a deadly curse.

No, Leksander had always been the steadfast brother. The one who would persevere with a cool head, think through the options, and perform his duties to the best of his ability. He was the one who talked Lucian out of his suicidal despair after losing his mate. He was the one who stayed by Leonidas's side as he dared to hope for release from his curse. But now, stuck between his own impossible desires and immutable duty, Leksander could see nothing but bleakness ahead.

Five hundred years of it.

And that was the best possible case. That was assuming he could seduce a fae queen or a willing human to fall in True Love with him and bear his child. A loveless pairing for him, but one that would extend his life.

And give him a child.

That… Leksander sat up, suddenly, water still steaming off his dragon-hot body. *That* was the silver lining for his silver dragon. Not simply that having the child would extend his life… *but that he would be a father.*

It wasn't the kind of thing he'd ever considered before. But now that he'd held little Larik, his father's namesake… now that he'd helped birth baby Thorn… there was a magic to those tiny beings that renewed the spirit. Every dragon in the keep felt it. Each child was a miracle, and that held a power all its own.

Leksander may not truly love the woman who would bear him a child, but there was no doubt in his mind that he'd love the child himself.

And that was enough.

He rose up, magicked away the water still clinging to his body, and conjured clothes.

In that strike of insight, he had gained a new urgency. This mating wasn't merely about seducing a woman and saving the treaty—it was about choosing a mother for his son. A strong mother, one who could survive an immortal pregnancy. A soft-hearted mother who would love his son

—and by necessity, Leksander himself. A woman brave enough to leap into an unknown future where Leksander would catch her and give her anything her heart desired.

No matter his personal feelings, any woman willing to do this—fulfill the treaty, protect humanity, risk a dangerous pregnancy for love—would be worthy of his utmost respect. He would cherish her, and the child they made together, all his days.

Maybe it wouldn't be love. But it would be close enough.

With renewed determination, he strode through the halls toward his lair. By those measures, how did mating with a fae queen stack up? His brother was right that the child would be fantastically powerful. The treaty would renew with a conviction that would cement the Summer Court as their permanent ally and protector of humanity. If Nyssa's demonstration in the throne room was any indication, the sex would be unparalleled—given he'd been chaste for more years than he wanted to think about, that idea alone was enough to surge up his dragon with a wanton hunger. But seducing the queen into a Love that was True?

The odds on that were long. Better than the impossibility of wringing love out of an angeling but still… not likely. That left finding a human woman in Seattle who would be strong and sweet and brave enough to endure the pregnancy. Not an easy task, but ten generations of the House of Smoke had managed it. He could as well.

He reached his lair and strode to his office. He had to rifle through his desk drawers to find his tablet, and it took another few minutes to install the WildLove app, but once he set up his profile, his enthusiasm took a sudden dip. How long had it been since he'd done anything like this? He set the tablet down and searched his memory for the last human he had bedded. Anger rumbled around his chest as every image he conjured was Erelah in some state of undress—all of which were entirely imaginary. He pushed those thoughts away. *Focus,* he scolded himself. But he could remember no encounters within the last century —all he could recall were his exploits as a young dragon in France, back when they were still living in the keep of his birth.

And then he remembered why.

Lucian had taken his mate in France, his first one —*Cara.* In a horror that haunted his brother for a hundred years, she and the baby died despite Lucian's efforts to save them, which included his own talons tearing into the body of his beloved. The trauma was felt throughout the House, and everyone went into mourning. Back then, it was supposed that Lucian was the *prototokos,* and his mating was the only one which could ensure the treaty. But his brother fell into a dark despair, and Leksander had spent many nights simply keeping watch from afar, fearing his brother might take his own life. Finally, it had been Leksander's idea to move the keep. Leave behind the memories, he thought, and perhaps his brother could heal. Words about duty were useless to a man whose heart was irrevocably broken. So they moved… and while Leonidas made every effort to include Lucian in his endless quests to bed every woman in Seattle, Lucian fought him at every step. Leksander implored him, but it was no use, and eventually Leksander realized that only time would heal his brother's heart… if it healed at all.

It was then that Leksander had stumbled upon an angel of light in a dark Seattle alley.

Erelah.

He growled and snatched up the tablet again. He would get nowhere if every thought led back to her. But at least he had solved the mystery of how long it had been since he'd lain with a woman. He remembered distinctly now the two times he'd attempted it—each a disaster in their own right. The first, he'd been so sex-starved that he'd barely made it ten minutes in before exploding. He remembered the disgust he'd felt. Not because he'd left his lover unsatisfied—*that* would never happen, not so long as he was *dragon*—but at the sheer emptiness of the act. He'd stormed around the keep for months before attempting it again, this time with some beautiful but hapless human he'd met in a bar with Leonidas. She was enthusiastic in bed, and they'd made a night of it, but the result was the same. A hollowness of spirit. A tarnish of the soul he couldn't wash away no matter how many plunges in the pool or scalding showers he took.

He was in love with Erelah, and there was no helping it. His beast had bonded with her, and any acts with another woman would be fraught with guilt and self-loathing. So he gave over to the idea, sought physical release with his own hand, and resigned himself to his fate.

All of which meant he had literally no modern precedent for seduction.

And seducing the Queen of the Summer Court? That was outside any dragon's experience, except for his great-grandfather ten generations back. Who happened to not survive long enough to advise anyone on his seduction techniques. So... not helpful except perhaps as a warning, which apparently, Leksander would not heed.

He shook his head at his folly and swiped open the WildLove app. No matter how empty the act, he should practice his skills on a human female before attempting to seduce a fae queen. And the elaborate dating game he had staged for Leonidas would take too long. Leksander quickly finished out his WildLove profile then swiped right on several choices. No blondes, thank you very much. No one with angelic blue eyes or softly curved cheeks or voluptuously full breasts—

His first answer pinged on his tablet.

The message was merely a hotel name and room. Direct. To the point. He should welcome this, yet... he couldn't seem to force himself to reply. Perhaps he should just show up at the appointed time? Surely courtesy dictated that he respond to confirm. She was red-haired, green-eyed, slender and tall... and she wanted to "ride your beast until you forget you're a man," which she helpfully added after the room information. And, if he were honest, that was precisely what he was looking for.

Yet, he still hesitated.

He gritted his teeth and forced himself to tap in a reply. *I will be there.*

It was a few hours hence, which gave him time to gather his wits... except another response, then two, pinged on the tablet. He set it on the desk and drew back. What had he gotten himself into?

Then an altogether different buzzing started up.

He took a moment to realize it was his phone.

Leonidas.

A quick glance at the time said he and Rosalyn must be near the end of their duties in receiving guests. Leksander's thoughts leaped to many undesirable things that could have happened. Demon invasion. Attack by rival dragon clans. A visit from the Angels. It wasn't as if those things hadn't happened already.

He quickly answered. "Do you need something, my brother?"

"Hello, Leksander! My brother, I'm sorry to interrupt you!"

What? "What's wrong?" His brother was speaking for

someone else's benefit. Leksander started toward the door of his lair.

"Just a small thing," Leonidas said over the phone, a hedge in his voice.

Before Leksander even reached the threshold, he surged out with his fae senses to sweep the keep. The wards were down around the throne room and the side entrance to it, but they were protected from the rest of the keep by another set of wards. Which only meant Leksander's fae senses ran smack into the barrier between here and there. "I'm on my way!" Leksander said quickly.

"That's all right, brother. I understand if you're busy."

What? Leksander stopped just outside his lair. "Is it the fae?" Maybe Leonidas needed him to gather the rest of the House before storming the throne room. Even then, it would be a difficult fight. But how dare the fae make an incursion now? Was the treaty worth nothing?

"No, no, nothing like that." Leonidas's voice held concern, but not the kind that would send Leksander into a panic.

"My brother, I don't understand." He wavered between sending a general alarm through the House and just striding to the throne room himself to assess the situation. "Do you want me there now or should I bring more help?"

Leonidas sighed, and his voice dropped to a whisper. "I have two angelings here. Erelah is one of them. I don't know the other."

Leksander froze in place. His heart wrenched in a way that caused him physical pain. *"Why is she here?"* he growled out. He *specifically* told her he would handle this on his own... and now she was bringing *more* interference from the angel realm?

"They have a box for you. It's white and glowing, and I'm pretty sure it's angel magic."

Fuck. That wasn't something he could turn down. "I'm on my way." Leksander hung up the phone and strode angrily toward the throne room. Whatever she had brought—and *whoever* she had brought with her—Leksander would accept it and send her packing. It was a constant struggle to keep her out of his thoughts when she *wasn't* present. If she was truly his friend, as she claimed to be, she would respect his wishes. And right now, his fervent wish was for her to wink back through the transdimensional door that led to her faction's realm... *and stay there.*

He had other women to seduce—ones who might actually want to be with him.

When he burst through the throne room doors, all heads swung to him. His entrance was already dramatic, so he ignored the stares and whispers and just hurried down the middle of the long hall toward the front dais. Erelah was there, clad in some tight-fitting half-toga that ended in snug shorts instead of a draping skirt. Per usual, the white, nearly transparent fabric clung to and revealed her curves in a way that would be seductive... except for the innocence of any seductive intent on her face.

Which was shining with inexplicable delight as he approached.

Leksander ground his teeth and tore his gaze from her to the angeling standing at her side. Both of their wings were out, and they stood just in front of Leonidas and Rosalyn on their thrones. Baby Thorn nestled in Rosalyn's arms. The angeling was a male, and as scantily dressed and ethereally beautiful as they all were. This one had short, white-blond hair and blue eyes that steadily watched Leksander as he approached. The angeling's toga draped low on his hips and barely covered his chest, revealing a tattoo down his arm. Leksander frowned as he got closer and realized the tattoo was of a *dragon*. It was unusual for angelings to tamper with their bodies—something about being perfectly made by God—but for one to wear a dragon tattoo seemed doubly strange.

The angeling studied Leksander, just as he was sizing him up. The glowing box was cradled in the angeling's hands.

Erelah's excited voice drew him back. "Leksander, I'm sorry to interrupt you. Were you hunting for a mate already?"

It was all Leksander could do not to snarl. "I'm handling it. As I said." Leonidas was wincing in his chair, and Rosalyn's smile looked forced and painful. The entire keep was watching, and Erelah had to spill it out? That artless innocence he so often made excuses for or secretly thought was endearing felt like a slap in the face now.

"Of course, you are," the male angeling said, smoothing over the painful awkwardness. He bowed deeply to Leksander then held up the box. "I am Tajael. Markos has sent me with a gift and message. I hope the House of Smoke will forgive our intrusion, but our realm has a great and abiding interest in all the princes finding their True Loves and renewing the treaty."

Leksander eyed him. Tajael was unusually well-spoken for an angeling. "Of course, we welcome any gifts from the angels." As if they had a choice. But Leksander was trying to bring decorum back to the situation.

"I'm so pleased to hear that." Tajael stepped forward and presented the gift to him.

"Isn't this supposed to be for the new prince?" Leksander really didn't want to take the proffered box. Erelah looked stricken at his hesitation, which gave him such a disturbing reaction—a grim satisfaction at her

concern mixed with a painful longing for her approval—
that he resolved to just take the box and get this over with.

"Ah! The young prince." Tajael smiled in an openly
adoring way at the baby tucked in Rosalyn's arms. "We've
already bestowed our kisses upon the child." He turned
back, and his smile tempered to a smirk. "Not an easy feat
with a child so strong with fae magic. But the child is
basked in love and surrounded by the protection of the
treaty. He's not the one Markos is concerned for."

Leksander narrowed his eyes. "He needn't be
concerned."

"Of course." Tajael waved that away, giving the
impression he fully believed Leksander would easily find a
mate while simultaneously not giving an inch on the
concerned position of the Angels.

Leksander regarded him anew. This angeling was
skilled in human interactions and had some purpose for
being here beyond delivery of the box. "What is this
message you want to deliver?"

Erelah was keeping strangely quiet, eyes bright as she
let Tajael take the lead.

"First, if I may, the blessing." Again, he offered
the box.

Leksander reluctantly took it. Erelah beamed with
happiness, but it felt to him like he was holding a bomb.
Technically, this was a life-giving bomb, not a life-
destroying bomb, but power hummed through it and made
the runes jump along his skin all the same.

"This blessing is yours to dispense, prince of the House
of Smoke," Tajael said in a suddenly formal voice.
"Whosoever you deem in need of it—your mate, your
child, or even someone tangential but necessary to the
purpose of renewing the treaty."

"Thank you," he said stiffly. A blessing from Markos

helped save Lucian's mate Arabella when she was beset by demon poison, so Leksander would definitely use it if the occasion arose.

Erelah seemed unable to contain herself any longer. "Markos wants you to know that you may call upon him." She seemed to think this was a great honor.

"All right." Leksander wasn't in the mood to fawn over Markos.

Tajael nodded his encouragement to them both. "Markos was clear about the threat the fae may pose to your mating, Leksander. He assured me that I may use any powers I have—and call upon him if necessary—to ensure they do not interfere in this crucial matter."

"I appreciate that." Leksander tried to sound like he meant it, which he did, but the turmoil in his chest with Erelah being here was still keeping his words tight.

"To that end, I hope you'll allow me to remain nearby," Tajael said, his smile dropping into solemnness. "Erelah as well, of course. But I'd be honored if you would let me serve as a Protector during this critical time."

Leksander knew Markos's faction were Protector class angels, but this was just... *no*. "That's not necessary."

"I certainly hope so," Tajael said with a smile. "Yet, I would hate to take any chances with the young future-prince. Especially given how the fate of humanity depends on his successful birth."

Leksander clamped his teeth together. This was quickly sounding like it was non-negotiable. "I have an appointment in the city, so perhaps later—"

Tajael clasped his hands together. "Splendid! I hear the demon hunting in the city is especially good right now." He gave a small smile to Erelah. Her smile had vanished, and she was back to looking stricken.

"I'm meeting a potential mate." Leksander let the

words hang in the air and studied Erelah's face for any sign of jealousy or alarm, but she was just dashing looks between him and this Tajael person, as if she were more concerned about being excluded from the demon-hunting than anything else.

"Already meeting a mate? Even better!" Tajael said with a broad smile. He gave a nod to Erelah. "We'll clear out the neighborhood of demons and then stand guard for any more that might wander your way. At a respectful distance, of course."

Erelah nodded her assent quickly enough. Behind her, Leonidas was wide-eyed, no doubt at the news he was meeting "a potential mate." And if Rosalyn's eyebrows hiked up any higher, they'd fall straight off her head.

Leksander turned back to Erelah. *So...* he would fuck a human woman while Erelah circled overhead on her angelic white wings? *Not* how he'd envisioned this going, but if any act could convince his heart it had no chance with an angeling, that would be it.

"Very well," Leksander growled out, his words directed at Tajael. "We leave immediately." And with that, he turned his back on the two angelings and their vibrating hum of angel power, not waiting to see if they would follow.

With all their angel powers, they could beat him to Seattle anyway.

The trip to the city by air was short, and mercifully, neither Tajael nor Erelah attempted to mindspeak with Leksander in dragon form. Perhaps Tajael didn't know how. Maybe Erelah was having second thoughts about witnessing, even from a "respectful distance," while Leksander made another woman writhe in pleasure. And *oh* how he would make her writhe!

But, by the time they arrived, Leksander was convinced by the serious and determined expression on Erelah's face that his speculation was just that—a fantasy in which Erelah actually *cared* what he did with his cock and where he put it. He knew her too well. That look of tense excitement was for the demon kill. Perhaps also for "guarding" Leksander's tryst, as Tajael put it, since that was a step forward in Leksander fulfilling the duty Erelah had been endlessly insisting he must. She was concerned for all of humanity… not a single human/dragon hybrid like himself. At least, no further than the duty which befell him.

His disappointment in that ran deep. It was still *his* heart that needed to be convinced of its foolishness… and this was a grand, if messy and disturbing, way to do it.

They circled over the hotel where Leksander's Wild-Love date would arrive in about an hour, assuming she kept the appointment. He had no idea the hit rate on these things. It didn't take long for a demon-infected human to enter the five-block radius they were patrolling. Erelah dove for it first while Leksander and Tajael were left to follow. By the time they landed, Erelah had already grabbed the young man—he couldn't be over twenty—off the street, flew with him into an alley, landed amongst the dumpsters, and plunged her angel blade into his chest. All entirely cloaked, of course. The demon wail was ear-splitting, and the man's cries were muffled by her hand, but they could still be heard.

"She's exceptionally talented," Tajael said in a conversational voice, standing next to Leksander with his nearly bare chest and angelic toga.

Leksander didn't bother to answer. In fact, he ignored Tajael's presence as much as possible, focusing on the way Erelah's kill made her delicately pale skin flush, how she tipped her head back, eyes closed—that entrancing pose was precisely the one he used in all his best fantasies while bringing himself to climax in the cold loneliness of his lair. In an alternate world, Erelah would have that expression as he gave her an orgasm like no angel ever had. And perhaps that was entirely the problem—the pleasure she sought wasn't the kind he could give.

The man she was saving went limp in her arms. Erelah yanked the blade free of his body and gathered him to her bosom like a lover.

"However, the best part *is* the kiss," Tajael said by his side.

Leksander flicked a look at him. The angeling was studying Leksander's face with an inscrutable expression. He schooled his face so what he was thinking wasn't so brazen upon it. But it was hard to maintain his disinterested exterior when Erelah was giving an open-mouthed, erotic kiss to the human in her arms. She was breathing life into him—Leksander understood that intellectually—but the flush of pleasure through both was unmistakable. The man's arousal scent flooded the alley, not to mention that he was now sporting an impressive erection. Erelah's face was likewise rapturous.

With a jolt, Leksander realized that, all long, he'd been watching her engage in what was essentially her most erotic act... and not from a "respectful distance" but up close and personal, like some indecent voyeur. Except Erelah had no qualms about flaunting it in front of him.

He was now even more determined to repay that flaunting in kind.

She finished her kiss, and her rescued human stumbled away, a look of longing on his face. It struck Leksander again that this casual human that Erelah just met had already experienced more first-hand pleasure at her hands than he ever would. That, and the heavy-lidded expression on her face was so clearly a post-orgasmic haze. Leksander's jealousy seethed so strong, he could barely contain it to the low growl deep inside his chest.

"I claim the next one!" Tajael said brightly, unfurling his wings and lifting out of the alley. Erelah quickly followed, and Leksander trailed after them.

For the love of magic... he didn't know if he could stand to watch *that* again. Erelah showing off all the pleasure Leksander could never touch would be the death of him.

By the time he caught up to Erelah and Tajael, the male angeling was already deep into giving his life kiss to an elderly woman. Leksander had to wonder at the prevalence of demons in the city. It seemed to be on a substantial upswing, something he only vaguely noticed when he was hunting with Erelah. Then, his thoughts had been too tormented and absorbed by his own dilemma—and trying to discern Erelah's heart—to notice the demons themselves. But in the cool observation of Tajael rescuing yet another demon-infected human, Leksander had to wonder what this escalation meant for the House of Smoke as guardians of humanity—in their hometown of Seattle most especially. Had the demons raged out of control while they were away in France? Was the rightful pre-occupation of the dragon princes with the need to mate giving leeway to the Winter Court to continue their plans unnoticed... or at least without resistance?

Tajael released the woman. The flush of orgasm on the elderly woman's face—she definitely enjoyed her life kiss from a handsome angeling in a nighttime alley—seemed to make her twenty years younger. Erelah stood nearby, an approving look on her face. Tajael stepped up to her and—

Leksander's mouth dropped open.

He didn't know what he expected, but Tajael grabbing hold of Erelah's cheeks and planting an open-mouthed kiss on her was *not fucking it.*

A volcano of anger and jealousy and flat-out *rage* surged up in Leksander's chest.

The kiss went on and on, and there was no doubt they were both enjoying it.

Immensely.

Fucking hell.

He thought—no, he was *certain*—that angels and angelings never fucked. Not each other, not angel-to-angel, or angeling-to-angeling or any combination thereof. Obviously, they fucked humans, on occasion, spawning the angelings themselves, but it was considered a great disgrace in their angel status. At least, that was the lie Erelah had told him. A lie laid bare by the erotic kiss on display in front of him. And they might as well be fucking—they were practically naked—Tajael's erection tenting out his angelic toga, and Erelah's nipples at fabric-straining perkiness.

She lied to him.

And somehow that was worse than not caring.

Just as their kiss broke, Leksander muttered words that were bitter ash in his mouth. "I'll leave you two alone." And he meant every word, now and forever.

With his own sweep of wings, he shifted to dragon and lifted fast and hard out of the alley, speeding up over the towers of the city and heading for his keep. He couldn't stomach meeting his WildLove date now, not with any chance of Tajael and Erelah nearby. But the trip had accomplished its purpose regardless.

A highly educational purpose.

It wasn't that Erelah was *incapable* of love… it was that she was incapable of loving a lowly and decidedly *not* angelic dragon-fae hybrid.

Which made him certain of his next destination.

The Summer Queen's bedchambers.

Chapter Five

"Erelah? What is this?" Tajael's voice floated across the training room.

He'd finally found her. *Good.*

"Prepare to defend yourself." She said it quietly, but she knew he could hear. Sound carried well in a room made of crystal walls and crystal floors and held together with the magic of the Dominion. She strapped tight the bindings of her gloves at the wrist then gripped her blade overhand. Her wings unfurled, and she lifted into the air.

Tajael just stared up at her with concern. "I do not wish to spar."

No matter. She would draw his blood regardless.

Her warrior cry rattled the crystalline structure of the walls, her fury righteous as she flew, blade raised, straight at him. His wings reflexively unfurled, but it still took him a moment too long to leap out of her way—she nicked a feather, the pristine white marred by the scarlet red of his blood as it whipped through the torrent of her passing.

"Erelah!" he screeched in complaint, climbing aloft.

She banked and came around again. "You have

tarnished my honor!" she screamed as she bore down on him.

This time he was ready, waiting until she got close, then dropping below her and grabbing at her feet. She kicked his hands away, flipped head over heels, then sliced her blade across his chest on the way down, head first toward the floor.

He cried out, although it sounded unsatisfyingly like frustration, not pain. "Erelah, *stop it!* I can explain!"

She pulled out of her dive just before she would have split open her head on the floor, then she arced wide and climbed to the pinnacle of the training center again. She wiped his blood from her blade on the back of her glove then switched her grip to underhand. "Explain it to the tip of my blade." Then she charged for him again. He was fully across the empty training hall, but that just gave her time to build speed.

He braced for her, his own hands still blade-free. Why didn't he defend himself? Maybe because he knew he was *wrong* for what he did. It was *shadow angel* enough that he had forced the kiss—and a life kiss, no less, knowing full well she would be powerless against it—but he shamed her *in front of a friend.*

The fury of it drove her even faster, but when she reached Tajael, he once again dodged her, rather than facing the fight like an angel of honor. She banked and pulled up, but she was too close to the wall. Her own speed knocked her hard into it, stunning her and dropping her to the floor twenty feet below. She lost her blade in the tumult, and she landed with a loud *thump.* She took a moment to recover her senses, and she had to grip the wall to stand again. Her vision swam with darkness.

"Are you done?" Tajael shouted from halfway across the training hall. "Will you let me explain?"

She didn't need his explanation. She needed her blade and a few more good runs at him. She wouldn't kill Tajael—even *he* wasn't worth a mortal sin—but she would make him feel her anger and her pain in a few more strikes before she banished him for good from her sight.

Erelah stumbled around, blinking away the black dots swimming in front of her, searching through the bleary brightness of the crystalline floor for her clear blade.

After Tajael had foisted his unholy kiss on her, she'd come to her senses to see Leksander had rightly flown off in disgust. Anger boiled anew as she dropped to hands and knees to search for her blade. Just when the dragon prince had moved forward with finding a mate… just when he'd agreed to let her stand guard with Tajael in helping make that happen… Tajael ruined *everything*. For an angeling storied for his perceptive talents with humans, he'd messed up the entire thing… and with a repulsive act she couldn't begin to comprehend.

"Is this what you're looking for?" Tajael stood calmly about ten feet away, holding her blade.

She scrambled to her feet, growling her frustration. "An angeling is more than her blade." She sucked in a fast breath, and Tajael's eyes went wide. Then she let loose her siren, that screaming angelsong that knows no mercy, shaking the very foundations of magic and pulling it apart at the seams. Tajael dropped the blade and clutched both hands to his head, but she was light and song and power, mighty in her righteousness. She lifted up on magic power alone and spread her arms wide, her entire body given over as a harmonic, enhancing the angelsong's power.

Only when Tajael dropped prostrate on the floor, which was jumping and warping with her song, did she stop. As soon as it cut off, she was subject to the resonance, the waves of it bouncing off the walls and slicing back through her. It wracked her hard, dropping her to the floor as well and forcing her to scramble back and brace against the wall. Thus was the danger of angelsong—that it might rip apart the very one who made it

Quickly, though, it subsided, attenuating out into nothing but an ache inside her head.

Tajael shook his, side to side, a weary protest as he rose up from the floor. *"Holy angels of light,* Erelah." He peered at her, rubbing the back of his head. "I pity the fool who makes you his enemy."

"You are that fool."

"I am not." He gave a small smile, the kind that twisted her heart… because it was the same smile he'd always had. The kind and gentle smile he bestowed on everyone.

And *that* was what hurt the most—not the kiss or the shame, but that she lost two friends because of it. One who betrayed her, Tajael; and one who felt betrayed. *Leksander.* She knew what he must think. All those times she insisted on the purity and chasteness of angels and angelings—that they only ever were tempted by humans, and not by each other. *Which was truth.* Because angels of the light could not easily stand a touch, much less a kiss or other sexual acts. The life kiss Tajael used to overcome that natural repelling of angelkind-from-angelkind was some kind of cleverness born not of any Virtue. It was not an outright Sin, but it had all the appearance of one.

And what did that make Tajael?

No friend of hers.

He wiped the blade clean of his own blood. The trail of red across his chest was still fresh, but already healing. His angel nature was strong, so she knew he could take it, even as she took out her frustration. Then he turned the blade grip toward her and offered it up, flat on his palm. "If more sparring will allieviate your Wrath, then let's have at it," he said gently. "Far better than to have it trapped inside you, festering and turning you dark."

She stared dully at the blade, hesitated, then took it. Then she glared at him, but when he spread his arms wide, offering himself to her for carving up into small angeling pieces, she sighed in disgust and sheathed it in the holster strapped to her leg.

He nodded and said, softly, "You are far more angry than I suspected you might be."

"Is that what passes for an apology from you?" Her voice was still bitter, and in truth, she was far from forgiving. Far, far from it. In fact, it was possible she left forgiveness back in the human realm when she raged and fled to the safety of the Dominion, where her angeling powers would harm no one on accident.

"I am *not* sorry." Tajael stood before her, saying those words and daring her with those blue eyes of his to ask *why.* It was a game she did not want to play, and yet… her fury was such that she couldn't walk away from him, either. Even though that was what he deserved.

"Explain yourself," she said tightly. "Before I decide it was a mistake to sheath my blade again."

He flicked a look to her thigh where the blade was strapped but seemed unmoved. "Erelah, my friend, you are as righteous as any angeling I've ever known."

"Flattery will not fix this, Tajael." Her voice hiked up. "Only truth."

"And you shall have it." He squinted at her. "But I doubt you will like it."

"Patience is my least favorite Virtue, Taj."

"Then I shall not press it." A small smile glimmered on his lips then faded. "At first, I took Leksander's anger, back at the keep, as a simple frustration at our angeling interference in their dragon mating rituals."

"There is much of that," she conceded. "They are a proud people, and rightly so. The House of Smoke has a long history of righteousness."

Tajael tipped his head in acknowledgment of the obvious. "Yes, but that doesn't explain how he looks at you, Erelah."

She frowned and pulled back. "What do you mean?"

"I mean he does *not* look upon you as a friend."

"Of course, he does. We've been friends for many years—"

"Erelah." And the way he said it arrested her heart. Patient. Kind. But she was missing something. Something important. "He looks upon you as a lover does."

She blinked. Her heart, still thudding from the fight, pounded an insistent gong inside her chest. Her head shook in time with it, twitching its denial, but no words came out of her gaping mouth. Then finally, she whispered, "He does not..." but she couldn't finish the words. *Did he?* Did Leksander look upon her that way? The horror of it was creeping up on her like an eclipse sweeping over the land and shrouding everything in darkness.

There was sympathy on Tajael's face. "It is easy to miss. He hides it well. I suspect he has had to because..." He gestured to her with open hands.

"Because why?" she demanded, even though she knew. *Because she could not return that love.* Her faction was Chastity. She took a vow. She may struggle with the other Virtues, but at all times, Chastity was her bedrock. It was literally what made her an angel of the light.

"Erelah..." His voice softened, and he stepped closer. The blood still wept in small red tears from the gash on his chest.

Erelah couldn't tear her eyes from it. How could this be true?

"You didn't see it because you didn't want to," Tajael said softly. She looked up sharply and met his gaze. But there was nothing but Kindness there. "You wanted to be friends, and you knew that you couldn't if… if you knew he felt more."

Erelah let out a small gasp. Because Tajael's words rang with the clarity of truth. She *still* didn't want to know this! Because it changed everything.

"I'm sorry, Erelah." He frowned. "You didn't know, and truthfully, how could you? I suspect he only let it loose when it couldn't be helped. Like today, when you slayed that demon. The look on his face… I've seen it before, during my walkabout, and it never ends well. Not for our kind. Or theirs."

The horror came creeping back and seemed to envelop her mind, dulling it, making it thick with despair. "Why didn't you just… just *tell me*, Taj."

He nodded. "I thought of it. For a moment. Maybe even two." His frown came back. "I didn't want to cause you pain, but it's not just your heart at stake here. Or your wings. This is a prince of the House of Smoke. The *final* prince. He must mate with someone who can bear him a dragonling."

Something was breaking inside her. Something as hard and fragile as the crystalline floor underneath her bare feet. But she nodded because, of course, Tajael was right.

"You didn't see his face, Erelah," he said, and now his voice held the apology he refused to give before. "He would never have let you go. Not in a million years, and we don't have that kind of time. I knew your honor could take a little bruising. I knew I could stand to lose you as a friend. But the world cannot afford to lose Leksander Smoke to a doomed love affair with an angeling."

The breaking was sharp and tearing, and she wasn't

sure, but she thought something might be physically wrong with her. She pressed the heel of her hand to her chest, right above her heart, where it seemed she might be dying inside.

"I'm so sorry, E," he said.

She just nodded, dully.

"I had to…" He swallowed. "I had to make sure."

"So you made me a liar," she gasped, finally looking up at him, the pain inside threatening to bring on tears. *Tears.* She had only ever cried once, and that was only for joy… when Markos had blessed her and accepted her into his faction.

"I made you *unavailable,*" he said, his voice a little more stern. But he softened it immediately. "And a liar. And someone who never saw his love but easily enjoyed my kiss. It was wretched, and I'd gladly pay for it with more strikes of your blade. But it was *necessary,* Erelah. Not all our choices are easy or righteous."

Somehow that only made it worse. That there couldn't be a way through this that was pure and righteous in all things.

"I… I need to…" The pain in her chest continued to grow. The darkness was encroaching on her mind. She swallowed to clear the thickness in her throat. "I need some time to… understand this."

"Retire to your cell," he said solemnly, stepping back. "I'll ensure no one disturbs you."

By which Erelah was sure he meant he would go straight away and tell Markos all that had transpired. And if the House of Smoke needed anything further from the angel realm, Markos would not be calling on *her.* Or perhaps even Tajael.

Her friend had risked much to make this happen.

To save the world from a mistake she had made.

She nodded, and with wings dragging limp on the floor behind her, she willed her feet to move toward the door. Toward the safety and security and normalcy of her cloistered cell. Toward a future that suddenly was tilted sideways and uncertain…

Except for the fact that Leksander would never again be part of it.

Chapter Six

LEKSANDER POUNDED ON THE DOOR TO LEONIDAS'S LAIR.

When he got no answer right away—which, to be honest, was only about two seconds—he pounded harder, nearly denting the bronze dragon relief draped around the edges as he gripped it. Only when he'd waited an interminable amount of time, fuming that his brother wasn't answering, did reason take hold.

He checked the time. It was nearly ten.

And his brother had a newborn baby.

What on earth was he doing?

Leksander stepped back and scrubbed his face. He'd nearly broken the speed of sound flying back to the keep, all on an urgent mission to visit the Queen of the Summer Court *now*. His fury should be directed at Erelah, but there was nothing to be done there, and besides, she was always on him to "do his duty." So he was determined to bury himself in some sizzling hot sex, the kind he'd been denying himself forever, all for some hopelessly stupid obsession with an angeling who wasn't even what she pretended to be.

She lied to him.

It ate through his gut all the way home, and by the time he folded his wings and dropped into the keep, he was hollowed out inside. There was nothing left but rage and a driving need for sex. He had no idea what hours they kept at the Summer Court, but the queen wasn't sleeping anyway, he was sure of that. She was getting off with some dragon—Dirk was his name—but Leksander was ready to pull rank and take a turn.

Very ready.

Just as he decided he was a fool—not to mention inconsiderate and generally an asshole—for pounding on Leonidas's door and probably waking the baby, and that he should slink away and find some other way to contact the queen, the door creaked open.

Rosalyn stood in her pajamas. "Oh, hey, Leksander. You're back already?" She frowned and rubbed her eyes.

"I'm sorry, I shouldn't have woken you." He really should just leave now.

"No, it's okay." She backed up and opened the door. "Come on in. I was just catching a little shut eye while Leonidas watched the baby. Have to sleep when I can. He's still getting up all hours of the night."

"I really shouldn't…" But he desperately wanted to talk to his brother, just for a moment.

"Don't be an idiot." She waved him in, so he complied.

Leksander followed her into the great room of Leonidas's lair—his and Rosalyn's now, he guessed—where his brother was walking a slow circuit around the room, gently bouncing baby Thorn and singing. Leksander was so arrested by the sight, he stopped halfway into the room. The song was ancient and in dragontongue—Leksander recognized it instinctually, the way one knows something they have no direct experience with. Like the idea that deep water is dangerous. Or that a mournful cry signals danger. Only this was an instinctively *soothing* sound, one that said—*you are home; you are loved.* It snuffed out his anger and made the hollow inside him whistle even more empty and cold.

He shook that off. He couldn't afford to be sentimental, not right now. What he needed *right now* was a revenge fuck, and he figured the Queen of the Summer Fae was perfect for that.

"Where is Dirk?" Leksander asked, walking the rest of the way into the great room, but keeping his voice hushed so as not to wake the baby.

"Dirk?" Leonidas asked, puzzled, as if Leksander had asked whether the moon was blue today. Then his brother scowled at him. "What happened to you? I thought you were..." He shrugged, as though he really didn't know *what* Leksander was doing in the city.

Which was exactly his thought.

"I've decided I'm going to seduce Nyssa." The words felt hollow, so he poured some of his anger into them. "If nothing else, I'm going to give her a hell of a ride."

Leonidas's eyebrows hiked up, and he dashed a look to his mate.

Rosalyn was scowling. "Are you sure you're all right?"

"No." Leksander's voice was far too bitter, and he needed to rein that in. "I'm not fine. I'm angry. I'm upset. I'm fucking *pissed.*" He sucked in a deep breath and tried to get hold of himself. Or at least channel that anger into something aggressively sexual. "And I'm going to *use that.*"

Leonidas still looked surprised, but now he was nodding. "That just might work."

"So where is Dirk?" Leksander asked, his voice rough. "Because if he's still in her bed, he's about to get kicked out."

"Okay." Leonidas handed the baby over to Rosalyn. "Give me a moment. I'll see what I can do." He stepped back but didn't go far. Then he closed his eyes and clasped his hands together, extended in front of him. His runes rushed down his arms and danced around his wrists. Leksander watched as he summoned the fae court, taking down the wards around his lair and reaching into magic space. He'd seen Leonidas do it before, and Lucian had once as well, and Leksander was sure he was capable of it, given he was stronger in his fae magic than either of them. But his agitation was too high at the moment.

And he was in no mood to calm the fuck down.

Rosalyn watched her mate warily.

"Maybe you should take the baby to another room," Leksander said as gently as he could in his agitated state.

But she nodded readily and hurried off to the bedroom down the hall, the guest room that had quickly been repurposed into a nursery when they returned.

Then a soft pop sounded, and the air seemed to overpressure for a moment, but a male fae appeared at Leonidas's side. The pointed ears and ethereal good looks were indications enough, but Leksander recognized this particular fae as Kalen, the queen's minion and, according to Leonidas, her lover. He had long red hair, with a thin braid on each side, bright green eyes, and runes writhing angrily across his nearly bare chest.

"The queen is *indisposed*," he spat. "Don't bother her—"

"She can make time for me." Leksander stalked forward, quickly coming face-to-face with Kalen. Leksander's own runes scurried across his skin, and the air pulsed with the power rolling off this fae. Regardless, Leksander demanded, "Take me to her."

Kalen's face twisted with an arrogant disgust. "Know

your place, prince of the House of Smoke. My queen will summon *you* if she has need of you." Kalen didn't seem to think the chances very high on that.

"She has a member of my House," Leksander growled. "She will return him immediately, and I will take his place."

Kalen's disgust turned into a frown that looked slightly alarmed. "What is the meaning of this?"

Leksander ignored him and turned to Leonidas, who was still locked in his summoning stance. "Call her again," he ordered. "This servant of hers is useless."

The fury on Kalen's face rolled through the air like a heat blast. He made some kind of inarticulate sound of anger then turned and disappeared in a flash of light.

"Well, *that's* a dangerous game," Leonidas remarked quietly. "I hope you know what you're doing, my brother."

Before Leksander could respond, Kalen was back... with Dirk's arm gripped in his hand. He shoved Dirk away, and the hapless dragon stumbled and nearly fell to the floor. He managed to grab an edge of the couch and remain standing. It looked like Kalen had ripped Dirk straight from the queen's bed and through the transdimensional window between the fae realm and the human world. His face was flushed, he was naked, and his cock was hard and dripping.

"My lord," he rasped out. "Have I done something wrong—" He was cut off by Leonidas conjuring clothes to cover him and signaling him to keep quiet, which he dutifully did.

The disgust was back on Kalen's face. He looked down his nose at Leksander. "The queen will now allow you—"

"You talk too much." Leksander stalked up to him and stared him in the face. "Take me to her."

Kalen's fury hummed the air with power again.

Leksander thought maybe he had already overplayed his hand—this fae could swat him like a bug if he chose—but then Kalen just gripped his shoulder and wrenched him through space and time.

It was momentarily dizzying, and Leksander had to blink twice to adjust his eyes to the change in scenery, but Kalen's rough shove away from him brought back Leksander's senses. He was standing in a vast room with hazy yellow walls and a carpet of grass. Vines dangled from the ceiling, diaphanous butterflies—or sprites as the queen had called them—flitted through the air, and a whole fleet of couches and beds surrounded the large, snow-white bed in the center. It was ancient in design, four posts with gauzy netting pulled back, and in the middle of its vast white sheeting sat the Queen of the Summer Court.

Naked.

Kalen dropped his voice to a growl. "The moment my lady wishes me to remove this trash—"

"That is all, Kalen." She waved him away, and Kalen disappeared so fast, Leksander wasn't sure if she had banished him with her magic or if he'd beat a voluntary retreat.

A slow, amused smile spread across the queen's face. "Curious, are we, dragon prince?" She was even more breathtakingly beautiful without the elaborate silver dress she had worn to the throne room. Her breasts were high and proud and flushed with what looked like small red bite marks. Her silver-white hair fell across her chest but didn't cover it, falling down her back as well and pooling on the bed. She sat on her heels, her knees slightly spread, and her sex was bared and obviously ready for attention.

Attention Dirk had no doubt been giving.

Leksander was tempted to magick away his clothes and

simply dive between the queen's legs, but this seduction, if it were to work, would need to summon more than just an orgasm or two. He kept his clothes on but stepped up onto the bed, stomping across the white sheets with his boots until he reached her.

Judging by her wide-eyed look up at him, he was piquing *her* curiosity. *Good.* He reached down and grabbed a fistful of her long-flowing hair, tilting her face up. Her lips parted, and he could see the hunger in her eyes surge.

"A queen deserves better than a lowly dragon of my court."

"Do I?" she breathed.

He wasn't yet touching her skin—he knew the effects of *that* from watching Dirk melt in the throne room—but she seemed entranced by his little play of dominance. The energy rolling off her was intense.

He held her head firm. "You deserve someone who knows just how to love you." Then he lightly brushed the thumb of his other hand across her lips. The effect was instant and intense—a wave of knee-weakening pleasure washed through him, and his cock instantly sprung to life. She must have felt it, this head-swimming vertigo of plea-sure, because she sucked in air across his thumb, and her mouth opened further, inviting him. She was at the right height to take his cock... but not yet. He still had on his clothes, but those were easily magicked away. No, he needed her *wanting* it far more before he actually gave her anything.

He pulled his thumb away, breaking the contact. His body had gone so long without—and he'd never felt *anything* like this—just that one brush was nearly intox-icating.

"So different..." she breathed. Then she licked her lips

and peered up. "That lowly dragon didn't have your magic, prince of the House of Smoke."

His magic? She must mean his fae blood. The original dragon who seduced a fae queen—his ancestor—did it without fae magic in his veins. But Leksander's fae blook must add power to that pleasure-drenched connection.

He bent down, still gripping her hair but now bringing his lips close to her face. "I haven't made love for a hundred years, Nyssa. You aren't going anywhere for a while." Then he brushed his lips across her cheek. Like his thumb across her lips, it flooded him with dizzying amounts of pleasure. His cock strained against the royal trousers he still wore from earlier in the day.

Her gasp was followed by a shudder when he didn't pull away. When his lips reached hers, he nipped them instead of kissing then pulled slightly away, breathing in her face. "Your mother took a royal dragon to bed. It nearly broke her Court. Are you sure you want to play with this fire?" Given she could toss him across the room with her fae magic, he wasn't doing anything she didn't like. But he was asking for more than just a fuck, and in a manner which he hoped she would find impossible to resist. *Did she want to risk taking him to bed?* It was rebellious. Naughty. It broke every convention and pulled at the taboos of their joint history. Not to mention, the King of the Summer Court might have an opinion... although it was well known that the Queen ruled in Summer just as the King ruled in Winter.

She could have Leksander if she wished.

With just the tip of his tongue, he tasted her lips, and the contact made her eyes drop closed. He drifted away from her mouth, skimming her jawline, not touching her with his lips, but dashing his tongue out in a steady beat of pleasure that pulsed through them both. His cock was starting to ache. He could think of worse fates than losing himself here. It would be empty of love, but fulfill every other need he had.

He pulled her head back further, opening her neck to him. This time he roughly seized her breast, holding her tight between both grips while he worked down her neck with small, erratic licks, each a little longer than the last. Her nipple drew tight against his palm, literal sparks of magic leaping between her flesh and his. When he reached her shoulder, he bit into it hard, as much to release the tension coiled tight in his belly as to give her pleasure.

She gasped.

"Answer me, Nyssa," he growled into her shoulder. Then he released his hold, his hand on her breast and his mouth against her shoulder, leaving only his grip in her hair as he rose up to her face again.

The contact was gone, taking its opiate of pleasure with it.

She whimpered deep in her throat. "Again," she breathed, eyes still closed.

He tugged harder on her hair. "Answer me."

Her eyelids fluttered but only opened half-mast. "I want you in my bed, dragon prince."

The pleasure that flushed through him was even more powerful than the magic touch. *Satisfaction.* He could please this fae queen, play her games, play her *body*, and she would want all of it. She would *beg* him for it. His touch. His cock. His magic. She would *want* him... unlike an angeling who wanted anything but him.

The intrusion of Erelah on his thoughts made him growl.

He wrenched Nyssa's hair back so hard he pulled her halfway to the bed. Then he grabbed hold of her breast again and pressed her back, crushing her with his body to the feather-soft whiteness of the spread. His cock strained against his clothes, and he ground their rough hardness against the creamy softness of her skin. Her moan was exquisite and just the salve he needed. Her aching need for him was a balm for the wrenching pain inside.

Nyssa *wanted* him. He could give her something no other being could—a magical pleasure that mere fae could not, nor a simple dragon. For he was *both*. And the pleasure he could bring was unparalleled. Nyssa would have everything Erelah never would want from him… and Nyssa would beg for it, whereas Erelah would only disdain him. Her high-and-mightiness, her angelic purity, was too good for the likes of him… but *Nyssa* understood.

And she craved everything he had to give.

"More," she begged.

He was lighting a line of pleasure with the tip of his tongue across her cheek while rasping her body with the coarseness of his clothes plus the hard muscles and cock buried underneath. He kneed her legs apart to grind the bulge of his cock against the nerve center between her legs.

"Yes!" She arched into him.

"Tell me you want this," he commanded as he slowly traveled the length of her body.

"No more teasing, dragon prince." She bucked against him.

He grinned and pressed her harder into the bed. His lips brushed against her neck. *"Say it,"* he breathed against her skin.

"For the love of magic, dragon, *I want you.*"

"What will you give me, Nyssa?" His whisper haunted her neck, sliding down to her collar bone.

"Anything."

"Anything?"

"Yes." She was breathing hard underneath him.

He worked hard to keep his voice cool. "I want *your love.*" He dragged his tongue across the rise of breasts.

"Yes." He could hear her heart pounding.

"All of it," he breathed against her skin, ghosting up toward her neck again. "Everything you have, Nyssa. I want it all."

"All my love." There was a catch in her voice.

It spiked through him. *She meant it.* There was something… something *broken* in her that made him flinch. But he continued on, sliding against her body until his lips brushed her ear. *"And a child,"* he whispered.

She gasped then shuddered as he bit into her neck just hard enough to electrify them both. It was too early to ask, and she wasn't answering, and yet… she hadn't said *no.*

He renewed his grip on her hair and pressed her, with his body and his words. "I *need* it, Nyssa," he panted, anger stiffening his words and every part of his body. "Give me what I need, and I'll give you everything you want."

She bucked against him, but it was a shuddering, gasping kind of motion. Like she wasn't entirely in control of her own *need*… and he knew that feeling all too well. He restrained her, held her down, fought against the rebellion of her body against whatever was going on in her head.

And then she released a long, slow breath. *"A child,"* she said in the tiniest voice.

Yes. "Say it again." He bit down on her earlobe.

She arched into him. "Take me," she gasped. *"Leksander, please."*

Good enough. He closed his eyes and nuzzled his face against her jaw. More than good enough. It was more than anyone had ever given him, and he'd only gotten started with her. His lips brushed her neck, surging even more of that magical pleasure-rush through them both. "I'll give you everything, my love," he whispered, but it made him wince. He kept nuzzling her body, but there was only one woman he had ever wanted to call *my love*. Only one he'd said those words to in his fantasies, the sexual ones where he climaxed calling out her name and the tender ones where all they did was touch. Hand to hand, lips to lips. He'd pictured this moment a thousand times, and always it was a blonde beauty with wings spread beneath her and curves that could make a man cry.

Erelah.

Only after he'd pulled in a breath did he realize he'd said that out loud.

The queen's body stiffened underneath him. A split second later, he was blown from the bed, sailing through the air, and lashed by the hanging vines which quickly wrapped around him and held him suspended in the middle of the room.

It all happened so fast, he barely had time to suck in a gasp of surprise.

But when Nyssa rose up from the bed, naked, hair fanned in all directions, arms spread wide and fury on her face… Leksander *well and truly* understood his mistake.

"Who is this… *Erelah?*" Nyssa floated through the air, like a terrible goddess of wrath.

"No one," he said, eyes wide. The vines tightened, threatening to both tear him apart and squeeze him to death. "Nyssa, wait!" He thrashed against their hold as one snaked around his neck. Dragons were extraordinarily hard to kill… but the Queen of the Summer Court could easily accomplish it in any of a hundred ways. And given the treaty was established by magic from her mother… Leksander had the sudden, desperate, and terrifying thought that she might be one of the few who could kill him by her own hand.

"*Who is she?*" The boom of her voice shook the vines

and the couches and even the floor rippled under its power.

But the death-strangling halted momentarily. Enough for him to breathe. "She's just… she's just someone I love." He couldn't even bring himself to put it in the past tense. Because he knew that wasn't *truth*, and Nyssa would brook nothing else from him right now. "Someone who doesn't love me back," he added, hoping that might help.

Maybe he would be too pathetic to kill.

For a moment, her face contorted into some unidentifiable emotion—something like hopelessness? Definitely pain. And then the fury came raging back. "Kalen!" she screamed, and it shook the walls.

The red-haired fae appeared in an instant, looking alarmed.

Before he could get a word out, Nyssa stabbed an accusing finger at Leksander. *"Take out this trash."* Her growl was a thunderstorm clawing the air.

Kalen disappeared and reappeared at Leksander's side. The fae gripped his arm, and an instant later, they twisted through space and time to land back at Leonidas's lair. But Leksander's boots barely touched the ground before Kalen grabbed him by the throat and hoisted him in the air. Leksander struggled against it, but it was like being choked by a mountain.

"The only reason you live, *beast,*" Kalen hissed, "is the treaty. If I could kill you, you'd be *ash.*" Then he flung Leksander against the bookcases lining the wall, breaking shelves and raining down many books and Leonidas's collection of bronze sculptures.

Kalen turned and disappeared.

Leonidas came running from the nursery, skittering to a stop when he saw Leksander slumped on his carpet amidst the wreckage he had caused.

"So… I'm guessing that didn't work out so well?"

"I'm still alive." Leksander hung his head. His best chance, and he blew it. All because he couldn't get *her* out of his head. He grimaced and peered up at his brother. "I wouldn't recommend going to the Summer Court for favors anytime soon."

Leonidas nodded and gave him a hand up. "She's… complicated. Nyssa, I mean."

"Yeah." He winced as he brushed debris from his shirt. "And I'm a fucking idiot."

Leonidas tipped his head in acknowledgment, which just made Leksander shake his head.

"I'm done with immortals," he said bitterly. "Starting tomorrow, it's nothing but human women for me."

"Now you're talking," his brother said with a fervent nod.

Leksander tried to feel his brother's enthusiasm, but there was nothing left inside him. Just an emptiness that would never be filled. He needed to find a way to cope with that, to move on… before it kept him from doing his duty. In *spite* of Erelah.

Leksander dragged his ass back to his own lair.

Chapter Seven

Erelah's cell was made of magic and light.

It was beautiful in its barrenness. Tall and narrow, the room had only a rolled mat for a bed, now tucked in a drawer, undecorated walls to ease the mind toward the light, and a perch near the ceiling from which one could hang and stretch one's wings on occasion.

Which was where she had been for the last hour.

The blood had rushed to her head, and the pressure had dulled her mind. Her heart also slowed to an almost reluctant thudding presence that made itself known in her temples and helped to clear her mind. *To think of nothingness.*

Definitely *not* think about Leksander.

Not about a friend she'd known for nearly all her life, but apparently, didn't know at all.

The ache in her chest still remembered, however, and it was that which finally made her give up the perch and drop back down to the floor. Eschewing her mat, she simply sat on the cool crystal flooring, legs crossed, enjoying the momentary relief as blood dropped back down into her body and made her head light. It was almost as euphoric as receiving a blessing or slaying a demon, but this one was empty of the glory of those actual feats. And soon enough, it subsided and left her mind crowded with thoughts once again.

She'd been sequestered in her cell for a day, at least. There was no sense of time here, and the Dominion itself existed in a strange way separate from the human world of time, in any event. It was telling how long she'd been in the human world—how *attached* she'd become—that she wondered about things like whether it was day or night. Whether Leksander had returned safely to his lair. How much time had passed for him and how quickly he would move on to finally finding a mate who could give him the True Love he needed.

The pain in her chest was ever-present, like a giant glacier had cracked down the middle and gaped with an open and irreparable wound… but it occasionally cracked just a little more. The fissure grew wider and tore at her soul just an inch more. And each time, it was like breaking her heart anew. For it did not escape her notice that *he had told her.* His single word of affirmation haunted her now.

Have you ever loved someone?

Yes.

He had carried this secret for some time, and *Sins upon her,* she couldn't help the craving to know precisely, to the minute, how long that had been. When did it happen? When was the moment at which Leksander decided he loved her, and yet, also decided that knowledge must be a burden he alone carried? Months? Years? Was the entire time she'd known him premised on a lie?

A lie of omission still wounded.

She was very familiar with all the Sins, and of course, strove for Virtue in all things, but somehow she knew this lie was not Leksander's. The lie was *hers* in not seeing what was plain to Tajael in mere moments with them together. Lying to oneself about the nature of things is just the first step of many rapid ones along a descent into Sin.

So she would have the truth, and only the truth, no matter the pain, from now on. That was the vow she made to herself the moment she entered her cell for contemplation.

But it was not so easy a task.

The practical matters were simpler, and Tajael had done her a favor here, as she'd finally come round to seeing. Leksander needed to fulfill his duty, and as his friend, Erelah's greatest joy would come in helping him do that. But in reality, because he had somehow fallen in love with her when she was busy ignoring the danger signs, she was, in actuality, standing in the way of Leksander fulfilling his duty. Tajael had taken it upon himself to act—Kindness and Charity were his strongest Virtues, after his vow to Chastity of course—so this didn't surprise her, once she thought it through. Tajael had perceived the problem in an instant, and he sacrificed himself to take action to right it. He was blameless in all of this. Moreover, he spared her from having to take such an action herself, if she could even bring herself to do it.

If she were truthful—and she had vowed to be—she knew her weakness was there. She probably would have fled. Then, on further consideration, she would likely have taken her life to remove herself from Leksander's fixation. The way must be cleared for the next princess of the House of Smoke, and if Erelah's own life could be given for that cause, she would not hesitate. Not even now, if it would help. Humanity was at stake, and one angeling's life was of no consequence by comparison.

That act... she could envision it happening. It would have spared her honor, but what effect would it have had on Leksander? *This...* this was where her mind kept stalling out, and the crack inside her kept growing wider. Because she *claimed* to be Leksander's friend, and yet, in all the time she'd known him, had she ever really thought of how he felt? The answer was obviously and painfully *no.*

And now she was reaping the wages of that Sin of thoughtlessness—a mix of greed and sloth that would never have happened had she even a reasonable amount of Charity or Kindness within her wretched angeling soul.

Suddenly, the walls of her cell felt too barren, too bleak. She surged up to her feet and released her wings. They crashed against the walls—the cell was hardly wide enough for the full span of them. She could never be a True Angel, never fully righteous, but an angeling's calling was to strive for that perfection as much as possible. It was difficult for someone tarnished by their very nature. She was *fallen* by birth, conceived by an angel who succumbed to the beauty of humanity and lost their light because of it. Only being rescued by Markos and brought to his Dominion gave her any hope of overcoming the deep conflict bred into her very soul.

And she had been so *fixated* on her own redemption she forgot her true purpose in the world—safeguarding humanity from the fae and demons and horrors that lay just past their seeing, just at the edges of their awareness. An eternal battle that must be fought or lost, daily.

What she needed was more of *that.*

A good demon hunt would clear her mind, center her in righteousness, and then she could see what her path forward might be. Maybe she needed to make apologies to Leksander. Maybe she needed to leave Markos's dominion and start over somewhere else. She could join Halo in the Patience faction—a suitable Penance might be to live under a commitment to her least favorite of the Virtues.

Now that Tajael had tarnished her in Leksander's eyes, she need not worry about removing herself from the turmoil in the House of Smoke. That was done. Now she needed to pay for her Sin and move back to saving humanity again.

It was literally what she was made for.

With that focus in her mind and a twist through time and space, Erelah left her cloister cell and dropped into the warm morning air above Seattle. Time had passed—it was nighttime when she was last here—but whether it was a day or three, she was uncertain. No matter. She would hunt, cloaked from the sight of humans, and then center herself in righteousness while she contemplated her fate.

It didn't take long to find a demon—it was disturbing how prevalent they had become. She knew Zephan, the fae prince of the Winter Court, was still actively recruiting the vampires to infect humans with these demon essences, and it seemed like the Angels should take issue with this—they should fight to stop it, if nothing else!—but she understood the fixation on the House of Smoke at the moment. Without them, the fae would be free to raise demons capriciously and not merely the possession kind which might give a false sense of power or purpose to the humans they infected. Without the treaty, the fae would overrun the world, and humanity would fall into a terrorized war zone or perhaps an abject poverty as demons rampantly destroyed peace once and for all. If that happened, she would see about training for Warrior class. It wasn't often that angelings could switch classes, and Protector class was the most useful during normal times, but if war broke out, Erelah would take the chance of falling to Wrath to be on the front lines.

Spurred by that thought, she dove down on the hapless demon-infected man whose scent she had caught three blocks away. Scooping him off the street in broad daylight was a trick, so she waited for that fraction of a second when all eyes were turned away then snatched him up and carried him to the roof of a nearby building. Cloaking them both, she muffled his cry as she slipped her blade into his side, forcing the demon to tear itself from his soul or face extinction. The glory and righteousness that surged through her as the demon fled filled her with certainty—Warrior class was where she belonged. If there was no war, then she could stand guard with the others, training and waiting for the day. She was a young angeling with many hundreds of years of purpose still stretching ahead of her.

Once the demon was gone, the man slumped in her arms, exhausted. His life essence was ebbing. It was then that she truly looked at him. He was young—perhaps mid-twenties in human years—and strong in body with broad shoulders and muscular arms. But the demon had laid waste to him, probably driving him to self-destructive indulgences that depleted the man of strength even as his relative youth carried him forward with a sense of immortality. Still, he was beautiful in the way all humans were—shining with the potential that God blessed them with.

She grabbed hold of his face to better deliver the life kiss, then she pressed her mouth to his and *breathed*. The thrill of delivering a restorative energy to him washed pleasure through her body. His body stiffened against hers, as they normally did, humming with the same pleasure of *life* that she felt.

Then he grabbed onto her.

This occasionally happened, but not often.

Usually, humans rapt in the throes of a life kiss were rendered insensate—unable to do much in response, just absorb the pleasure and perhaps have a few involuntary bodily reactions. That was much the case when Tajael delivered his shameful life kiss to her. She was surprised, yes, but once the flood of angelic energy pulsed into her, all she could do was absorb it, take it in, and attempt not to swoon from the sensations. Tajael had made a show of kissing her as well—for Leksander's benefit, as she now knew—but it was just a wet slapping of his lips against hers. The true *kiss* came from the breath of life itself, and that was what she reacted to.

Humans were normally the same, but occasionally, they fight through the overwhelming sensation and react as lovers do—by kissing back.

This man was attempting such a thing, although his mortal strength was nothing next to her given angel powers. Yet he was grabbing onto her face and moving his lips against hers and trying to pull her body into some grappling match in which the full length of his body was pressed against hers... including a fully erect penis, the usual side effect of a life kiss in men.

It was annoying, and she struggled not to end the life kiss prematurely, before she had fully restored all the health the demon had drained from him. In that extra five seconds of fully-grappling kiss on the rooftop, Erelah couldn't help but wonder what Leksander would see—and feel—if he happened upon them now. Surely he knew what she was truly doing—she had told him often enough—but how would it look to a man who had slipped into the unfortunate and dangerous position of loving a creature of angelkind?

You didn't see his face, Erelah, Tajael had said. *He would never have let you go.*

Erelah released the man from her life kiss. He clung to her, as they often did, so as gently as she could, she pulsed power to repel him. He stumbled back on the rooftop, but thankfully far from the edge.

"Peace be with you," Erelah said, waving him toward a rooftop door where he could exit.

"But I…" The man stepped toward her. "Please don't leave. You're so beautiful."

His words were a strike against her heart. How often had she put on this display in front of Leksander, heedless of the effect it had on him? How fervent had she been, how full of her own pleasure and righteousness, while he quietly suffered by her side? What sort of wretch was she truly for these things? Tears threatened again, stinging the backs of her eyes.

"Go in peace," she forced out, then unfurled her wings and lifted from the rooftop.

She flew hard over the city, beating back the tears and renewing her purpose—*the hunt.* She would seek demons until exhaustion took her, then she would flee back to her cell and contemplate anew the proper Penance for the crimes of heartlessness she had committed against one of her best and oldest friends. And the danger she'd put the world in because of it.

It didn't take long to find another demon, and this one drew her like a magnet.

A child.

What vile beast would infect a child with demon? Especially one so young—she couldn't be more than ten—and now vulnerable as her demon caused her to wander the alleys in a section of Seattle long abandoned by the righteous businesses of the city, leaving only the drug dealers and thieves and petty criminals.

Erelah swooped down and wrapped her wings and her cloaking around the child before the base nature of the humans around her could surge up and attempt harm. The girl squeaked in surprise, but her demon was already lashing out at Erelah. She quickly drew her blade and slipped it into the girl. The thrashing of her young body against the cleaving of demon from her soul brought a heart-wrenching concern to Erelah as much as a sense of victory.

Then a flapping of wings behind her grabbed her attention.

What in heaven—a clear slash of pain cut off any thought.

Erelah dropped the girl and screeched as she rose into the air and twisted to see… *a shadow angel!* She scuttled back through the air, her wings grabbing at it to haul her aloft, but the angel of shadow, with his midnight wings and bared teeth, had looped high from his first pass and was bearing down on her fast. He shot past her again, striking her with his obsidian blade, and pain sliced through her wing, leaving feathers falling to the ground.

She surged up, powered by magic alone, and ignored the screaming pain in order to chase after her attacker. He banked sharply again, flying to the top of the narrow alley, then diving down again… *after the child.*

Erelah shrieked her anger and charged after him, only realizing the trap when the dark angel braked mid-air, not touching the child, but turning to face her *blade first.*

His dark weapon sunk deep in her belly as she crashed into him, knocking him free of the child but leaving herself vulnerable to his attack. She kept hold of him then flung him away, and his infernal blade went with him, but the pain was blinding and hot and liquid. It was like the weapon had pierced her soul, and it was leaking out. The shadow angel crashed into the wall of the alley, which stunned and dropped him to the ground next to a dumpster.

Erelah didn't hesitate. She dashed back to the child, and wrapping her in wings marred with blood, she twisted through space and time to return to the safety of her cell. The child cried out in fear and surprise, but her demon was gone, so she could survive in Markos's Dominion.

"You are safe," Erelah gasped out, but the pain struck her like a lightning bolt, and she struggled to stay upright. She looked down to see blood soaking her training garb, the same tightly-wrapped clothes she wore to fight Tajael an eon ago in the training room. A gash of scarlet red likewise tarnished the white of her wings. The wounds were colored with ashen gray as well—a result of the shadow nature of the angel's blade.

A shadow angel in Seattle.

No matter what Markos might think of her, no matter the state of things with the House of Smoke or her dishonor, this was something her faction leader needed to know.

"Come with me, child," Erelah said, holding her wound to keep more of the boiling-hot blood from leaking out.

"There's an angel we must see."

Chapter Eight

THE JAZZ CLUB WAS LIT BY HER PRESENCE THE MOMENT SHE walked in.

Her white-fringed, straight-lined flapper dress couldn't hide those curves, but it was the way she moved that captivated Leksander. Careful, like every step mattered, yet boldly moving through the room without a care for the lascivious gazes that followed. Sultry with that sway in her hips, yet innocent of that as well. As if every doll walked the way she did. Bold. Confident. Like her dress was heavy battle armor, but she carried the burden well.

She was a study in contrasts.

Leksander couldn't take his eyes off her.

Then he reached out to taste her with his fae senses and found... angeling! Even more intrigued, he openly watched as she stepped past tables full of bruisers, a card game in action, and the stage where soulful music soothed Leksander's ache for home. He hadn't been long from France, but he would trade a good bottle of wine for all this whiskey, and his soul cried for some refinement in the rough-and-tumble town of Seattle, just getting started in this new world. Truthfully, he'd only come to the club tonight to convince his brother Lucian to leave the keep, while Leonidas was here for the same reason he always was—a female companion or two.

Leksander was just looking, not tasting, since Lucian had refused to come, but now, with this angeling… she caught Leonidas's eye as well. Leksander lifted his chin and gave his brother a nod to let him know he would watch over the creature. Leonidas could continue his pursuits. So Leksander finished his foul shot of whiskey and edged toward the far side of the club, where the girl—she looked barely twenty, although for angelings there was no telling—had been stopped in her sauntering by a group of men by the back door. They had the stench of ill-intent on them, but they were only human, not the vampires he'd routed from the city earlier in the week, nor the wolf shifters he'd chanced upon at the speakeasy. Leksander pretended to watch the horn player in his solo, but she never left the corner of his eye. So when she moved to the back door, surrounded by the pack of men, he was drawn as though a rope were leashed to his neck.

By the time he reached the fresh night air in the back, she'd already laid out three of them, and they weren't looking to get up soon. He'd never seen an angeling in action, just heard the story of them back in France, but the way she gripped the man she was kissing… no, not kissing, but something else… he was entranced. And she was drunk with it, releasing him and staggering back against the wall just to hold herself up. The man lumbered away, and Leksander quickly strode her side. Her head was tipped back, and she was breathing heavily, eyes closed and face awash in joy.

"Are you all right?" he asked, a little breathless with watching her. He'd given cause to women to make that face, but most who he had bedded were less expressive than this angeling even in the throes of the act.

She jerked upright and gaped at him. Then she moved fast and held a hand flat to his chest, pressed against his waistcoat and jacket. He would have flinched away with the suddenness of the movement, but his intrigue held him in place. Her eyes were still half-mast with whatever pleasure she'd been taking. And now that hazy, sultry look was only inches away. He fought the urge to simply kiss her, here and now, the only witnesses three passed-out human cretins who had displeased this angel in white. But he didn't want to end up on the ground like them, either.

Her eyes widened. "You are fae… and yet not fae. How is this possible?" The frankness of her stare tempted him to kissing again, but he wasn't that big of a fool.

"I am a dragon prince of the House of Smoke." Surely an angeling would have heard of the treaty that kept the immortal realm separate from the humans who populated the city… and the alleyway.

Her eyes widened. "My prince." Then her hand slid up from his clothes and cupped his cheek. She gazed into his eyes with her beautiful blue ones, and suddenly, her flapper dress melted away, leaving the revealing angel one she preferred, the strips of thin white fabric barely restraining her breasts. "My prince," she whispered again, rising up on her toes and bringing those lips tantalizingly close. His clothes were suddenly modern as well. He had one hand at her waist, the other luxuriating in the softness of her wild-flowing blond hair. Her lips were moving, but he couldn't hear her words, as if the world had gone silent, devoid of senses except for the strong beat of his heart, the intoxicating nearness of her lips, the silkiness of her hair… she reached to the back of his neck, slender fingers strong and insistent and pulling his ear to her lips. Then sound zoomed its way back in, and she breathed across his skin, "I want to give you a kiss, dragon prince." And he knew she didn't mean a life kiss, not the kind she'd given a hundred other men, but the real kind. The kind you give because your heart can't bear not to…

Leksander awoke with a start, air sucking into his lungs and his body lurching upright in his bed. He was drenched in sweat, and the ceiling of his bedroom bore fresh scorch marks.

His body raged with a tension not released.

Fuck. Even in his dreams, he was cut short before he could get any satisfaction. Just once. Just one fucking time, he wanted to kiss her in that surreal dream state where it seemed real. But only in his wide-awake fantasies did he ever bridge that gap between him and Erelah, the terminal distance that always held them apart. In those fantasies, he kissed her hard, fucked her harder, and she begged for more and more from him. In his wide-awake, pathetic beat-off sessions, she was willing and eager and wanted him above all things in any realm.

But his dreams weren't fooled. His subconscious knew the truth. And he should face that reality… and start a search for a human woman, one capable of the mating he was duty-bound to make.

He kicked away the tangle of sheets and swung his legs over the side of the bed. His head swam a little, and for a moment, he was back in the dream, at least emotionally. A nameless yearning hung over him, a perpetual frustration. He rubbed his temples to ward off the last vestige of the dream, but this was a real problem. He didn't want to screw up his next seduction by crying out Erelah's name when he finally climaxed at the hands of someone else again. This was too important.

He had to exorcise her from his mind as if she were a demon possessing it. And to do that… he probably had to see her again.

He rose up from the bed and stalked to the window, pressing both hands against the cool panes and staring at his pale reflection overlaid on the forested mountains below the keep. He wasn't sure he could keep his cool if he was actually in her physical presence again. Then again, maybe a good yelling fight would vent his anger. So she didn't love him. *Fine.* So she was into this other angeling, Tajael, even though she claimed angelings didn't fuck each other. *Fine.* He still needed to tell her, to her face, once and for all, that all these years, all this time they had together… it *meant* something to him.

Even if it didn't to her.

He had a real *friendship* with her if nothing else. And he needed to explain, in no uncertain terms, how that friendship could *not* continue. He would do what she insisted—find a mate who could love him—but he couldn't have her coming around or showing up unexpectedly with other angelings or even just flying in by herself. She needed to be *gone* from his life, and he needed her to know *why*.

That way he could count on her staying away.

And he could focus on moving on.

He shoved away from the window and dragged himself into the shower. He stayed there far longer than necessary, thinking this through. Did he just want to see her again? Was his messed-up head just making excuses? Maybe. But she'd been the sole focus of every fixation, every fantasy, for so long, it was like she was tattooed on his skin. And if she would never bear his mark for real, then he needed something dramatic to sever that tie.

He needed a breakup.

From a girl he'd never even kissed.

It was insanity, but by the time he hauled his ass out of the shower and dressed, he was certain. A big, showy, dramatic breakup, where he could tell her everything he felt. He could *finally* be honest. Then when she broke his heart yet again, simply because she didn't love him in return, he would be ready. *Because he already knew.* And then he could walk away with his head held high, knowing he'd said all that needed saying, and there was nothing more between them.

It would be hell, but it would finally be over.

He strode from his lair and headed for the throne room. He would need to let down the wards to summon her, and it was easier to do there, where he wouldn't have to expose the whole keep. Not that he minded having an audience for this. That might be better—if it was public, there was less chance of him losing his nerve and going back to her like he'd already done a dozen times. She was an addiction he needed to declare public abstinence from.

Still, he was relieved to see the throne room empty when he arrived.

If he were reaching through magic space to summon the Queen of the Summer Court, or even the Winter Court, he could access his primary fae magic to make the call. Angels were a different story. Normally, the House of Smoke would rather stay clear of them—their Dominion wasn't covered by the treaty, and they had their own agenda with the humans, although it was benign at worst and helpful at best. It had been centuries since demons had roamed the earth in significant numbers—even then, dragons and angeling slayers didn't work together so much as coordinate their territories. He and Erelah were unique in their friendship... and perhaps that was the problem. Dragons and angels were never meant to be friends.

Regardless, they'd worked out a way to keep contact so he could summon her when he wished. On her side, she could easily find him when she wanted to see him— moving through space and time was a gift of her angel blood—but for him to reach her was another matter. It wasn't as if they had cell coverage in Markos's Dominion of light. So she'd gifted him with a small piece of crystal. It appeared to be made of the same clear material as the structures in the Dominion that was Erelah's home, so he figured it was connected somehow. Regardless, he simply had to reach to it with his fae senses and place a call for her, so to speak.

Would she even answer? He wasn't sure. But she'd

never been the one to hold grudges against him, even when he lost his patience with her and stormed off.

So when Markos appeared in front of him in a flash of light, Leksander's heart sank.

"Prince of the House of Smoke." Markos greeted him with a small tip of his head. His wings spread nearly the span of the throne room, and he was barely dressed in a short toga, per usual. "Of what service can I be to your House?"

"I wish to speak with Erelah."

There was a slight hesitation, but Leksander saw it. "She is unavailable," Markos said. "What assistance can I provide?"

Unavailable? That was… odd. Was she actually going to avoid him? Or was Markos standing in the way? He had answered what was supposed to be a direct line to Erelah.

"This won't take long," Leksander said with a pinched look that warned Markos not to interfere if that was what was happening. "But I need to speak with her before I can proceed with finding my mate." Technically true. Markos could guess at why that would be.

The hesitation was much longer this time. Markos studied him for a long moment… and then just twisted away in a flash of light.

Leksander sighed. *Fucking angels.* Would it kill them to use common human courtesy? He waited, expecting Markos back any moment, but when the seconds stretched to nearly a minute, Leksander was ready to call him back and have it out with him.

Then Erelah suddenly appeared in front of him, a pulse of angel light preceding her.

"Erelah, I just wanted—" He stopped short when what he was seeing caught up to the prepared speech in his brain.

She was covered in blood.

"What the hell?" He stumbled to her side, hands uselessly floating the air around her. She had some kind of gash through her toga that nearly rendered it useless as clothing. The scarlet blood had drenched the flimsy fabric above and below. As he quickly scanned the rest of her, he saw her drooping wings were smeared with blood across one. "Erelah, what happened?"

Her face was always pale, but now it was a horrifying grayish color. *"Shadow angel,"* she gasped. "I'll be fine. Eventually." She stopped to swallow. "Markos said you had need of me."

"No." His chest felt like it was turning inside out. "You have need of me." He eased closer and slipped an arm around her waist. It was strange—in all the time he'd known here, they'd never actually *touched*—but she allowed it, putting an arm around his shoulder and leaning on him. "Come sit," he said, urging her toward the throne. She went with him, but he didn't like the weakness in her step. At all.

She eased into the chair, and he released her. "The diminishment will pass," she said, but not like she really believed it. "My light will fight the darkness. It will win out." The more she said it, the less he believed her.

"Let me heal you." He shifted a single talon and sliced clean across his palm. The blood welled up immediately.

"Leksander!" she hissed at him. "Do not injure your-self!" She was *pissed.*

"It's nothing." He scowled. "You know that. Now let me..." He moved to place his hand on her belly where the gash seemed still open and raw, but she cringed away. "Erelah, *dammit!* Let me heal you."

"It will..." She was staring at his weeping hand with wide eyes. "I will..."

"Yes, you will have a little of my dragon blood in you. And fae as well. But you're not just angel, you're human. In fact, it's the *human* part of you that's bleeding. You'll be fine." He wasn't entirely sure of this, actually—what the hell kind of wound was this?—but his need to *fix her* overwhelmed his mind and drove him on. Fucking hell, she was *hurt!* That wasn't supposed to happen. Not to her. Not ever. *She was an angeling.*

He fell to one knee before her on the throne and begged her with his eyes. "Please, Erelah, let me do this. I'll pull back if it hurts you in any way."

At that, she stiffened. "I am not afraid, Leksander."

That forced a smile through the pain. "I know."

She frowned, but she slowly moved her hand away from the gash.

Gently, so gently, because he wasn't at all sure how this would work, he slipped his hand past the blood-soaked tatters of her toga and flat against the gaping wound. He eased closer, just to be near her. She gasped and gripped his arm, but he could feel it, too. The extraordinary heat of her skin—she was hotter than any dragon to the touch! —and the surge of even more heat as his dragon blood mixed with hers in the wound. Plus his runes skittered down his arm and pooled at his hand. But that wasn't what had him releasing a slow, shuddering breath.

There was pleasure in their touch. Not just the fulfillment of some fantasy he'd had about the silky smoothness of her skin, but an actual surge of magic. Her angel power surged through the contact and rebounded with his dragon essence. The fiery touch of fae in his blood added a certain edge to it—as if their blood might fight instead of heal— but it wasn't too much. It just made the whole thing rage hotter and tighter in his belly.

Plus *it was working.* She tipped her head back on the

throne and held his hand to her flesh, gripping it now and keeping him flush as his magic healed her. The gray pallor of her face was replaced by a tinge of pink. Her eyes were closed, but her mouth was open, and air was working in and out of her chest. He could feel the wound stitching closed under his palm and the inky stench of darkness leaving her. Whatever this *shadow angel* was that had somehow wounded her, its presence was leaving. And the look of relief and breathless pleasure on her face was the most erotic thing he had ever seen.

When it was done—and he could feel it complete in the vibrating hum of wholeness under his touch—she sat up straight again. Her eyes were still at half-mast with the pleasure, and he couldn't help himself.

He leaned forward and kissed her.

Chapter Nine

Leksander's lips pressed to hers, and she didn't want
to flee.

That was the first revelation.

The next was how gentle he was. A tender touch of his
flesh to hers. The softness of his lips as they moved. She
was a rock by comparison—an unyielding, unmoving rock.
But this was nothing like Tajael's forced kiss, the one that
flooded *life* into her and rendered her senseless. And this
wasn't her ecstatic life kiss given to the countless humans
she'd brought back from the edge of death.

This was gentle and sweet and insistent.

It thawed the freeze that had taken hold of her, and
her lips moved with his.

They were kissing.

She put her hands to his face and held it, fingers
splayed. Everywhere they touched, there was a surge of…
something. Connection? Power? Her angel nature leaped at
the contact, and the wound in her belly, now sealed with
dragon and fae magic, sang with a need that somehow
tightened her everywhere and yet loosened everything. She

pressed harder against his lips, mimicking his movements. He made a noise that sounded like far-off thunder. Then his lips parted under hers, and his tongue swiped a hot line along her lips. She opened to him and parried back, her tongue fighting suddenly with his as to which could touch more and in which way and how strong... the rush of pleasure started low in her belly and rushed up to her face, suffusing her with a heat that might burn her if it blazed any hotter—

She jerked back and stared, wide-eyed and breathless.

Shame burned her face. She had been wanton and wild and lost in that kiss. She'd never done anything like it, never *felt* anything like it, and with a heart-stopping fear, she realized how dangerously close she'd just come to her Fall.

"Erelah..." Leksander's eyes were gleaming with joy.

What in the name of all the Virtues had she done?

Her face filled with the horror of it. She couldn't help it, but she could see him react to her change in expression.

It caused him pain.

Oh, Angels of Heaven, how wretched a creature she was!

"Erelah, it's okay," Leksander said, but of course, it was not. "I need to tell you something—"

"No!" She shoved her hand out, palm forward, to force him away. She pressed her back into the throne chair. If she could climb backward out of it without chancing to touch him again, she would. But she was trapped. "Do *not* say it." Her voice was ragged.

His pain twisted into anger. "I am going to say it! It needs to be said."

"Don't!" *Angels of light,* how could she fix this? *Truth.* That was the only way. "Don't say you love me. Don't say you want me for a mate! Because... because I *can't,* don't you see? I *can't* be that. You must know this."

He eased back from the throne and the tight spot where he had trapped her with his presence, and his shoulders slumped. His face held such pain, she would think he was dying, had she seen it on a human in a dingy Seattle alley. But this was all *her* doing. She had thought she could come here and just soothe whatever ailed him, but no… *she had kissed him!* No matter that he had started. She had reacted with pleasure and need and all the things that would only feed this desire he had for something between them. All while knowing what he felt!

There weren't words for that Sin, but she knew it was horrible.

The pain that lived on his face was all her doing.

"You should rightly be angry," she tried, but he cut her off with a look.

"Don't tell me you didn't feel that." And he *was* angry. "Don't tell me you felt *nothing* with that kiss."

She could say nothing of the kind. "That matters not!" She curled her fists and beat her frustration on the arms of the throne. Then she stood and towered over him, still bent on one knee. "I am *not* a suitable mate. I *cannot* do the things…" She struggled for the words, then gave up and dragged her gaze away from the hope in his pale blue eyes. The things. *Sexual things. Wild things.* More of those kisses that tightened her belly and sent her careening into a *need* like nothing she'd felt before. She would lose herself in that, and for what? She couldn't give him the True Love he needed to fulfill the treaty. It was impossible. She wrenched her gaze back to him as he rose up from the floor, now towering over her.

"Was it so horrible?" He was angry again, and that was where he should be. That was where she should have left it —his anger over Tajael's kiss forcing them both on the righteous path. Not this… this way led to ruin. For both of them.

"I cannot love you that way, Leksander! *I took a vow.*"

He frowned, and perhaps she had never explained the details of that. It had never been relevant—she took her vow long ago, yet *after* she met him. After she'd been drawn into that alley by men who were not demon-possessed, just gripped by their own darker natures. She had liberated them, giving her first life kiss to heal a human heart of its base nature… and then she met a man different from all the rest. Strong in Virtue and magic. As noble in purpose as she was called to be. Leksander intrigued her and uplifted her. For if a man who was dragon and fae could be *that* good of heart, then surely she, a tarnished angeling, could rise up and do the same. That night in the alley convinced her to return to Markos, to take her vow. And now… now she had done wrong by Leksander, leading him on with a kiss. A kiss that promised something that could never be.

"What vow?" he finally asked, his expression dark. He'd stepped back.

"My faction is Chastity," she said, drawing herself up and unfurling her wings. It was a declaration, and even the blood smear on her feathers couldn't tarnish that. "My leader is Markos. My devotion is to them. I am *angel of light*, Leksander—"

"*Half* angel," he whispered, but she heard it like a strike across her heart.

"Yes, *half,*" she cried out, raising her arms. "Half-breed. Half-formed. Conceived in Sin and forever tarnished. Yes, I am *half!*" Her voice had raised to angelsong.

Leksander winced under its power.

"Angels do not love as you do, dragon prince," she rasped out, her voice dropping to human levels again. "*I* do not love as you do. *I cannot.* I would lay down my life for you, Leksander, prince of the House of Smoke, but do not ask of me something I cannot give!" She stepped back, moving away because the torment on his face was more than she could bear. "Markos said you needed to speak with me before you found a mate." Her voice was half cry again. "Well, you have spoken, and so have I, and there is nothing more to be said. Go, then! Fulfill your duty. And I shall pay my Penance for what I've done all the days of my life."

His mouth fell open to say something more, but she turned her back and wrenched herself from his realm. The twisting of time and space brought her back to her cloister cell.

Alone.

And with that grace, that release, she fell to her knees and curled down until her forehead banged the floor. Her wings wrapped around her, holding her tight, and her arms gripped her belly as well. She felt as though she might tear apart. The fissure inside was cracked wide, and something had welled up from deep below. Primal and angry and irrepressible, it rose up and gushed out of her mouth in a screaming siren of angelsong. The sound tore at her, trapped with her in the cell, bouncing off the walls and slicing her mind and soul, scarring her like the strike on her body that Leksander had healed.

And when the song was spent, she wept.

Tears. Her first tears of pain and sorrow.

They would not be her last.

Chapter Ten

Pay her penance? For the love of all that's magic, what did that mean?

Leksander was tormented by Erelah's final words before she disappeared in a flash of light. He'd tried and tried to summon her with the crystal but either she broke it when she left or she was refusing to answer or… or Markos might be blocking him. But even that didn't make sense—he'd let her come the first time.

But what was this *vow* she made? Leksander knew there were factions in the angel world, but it wasn't like they were *warring* factions. It was more like *teams* the way Erelah had described it before, what little she'd ever said. He vaguely remembered that they even switched factions occasionally, so this idea that she was in a Chastity faction where she'd made a vow of… *what?* Swearing off sex forever?

Why couldn't she just switch teams if she found someone to love?

But she hadn't said that she loved him. Not in the least.

In fact, she'd said the opposite. That she *couldn't* love him. That she would die for him but *not* love him.

He raked his fingers through his hair, but no matter how hard he tried to make sense of that, there just wasn't any. He'd paced the throne room for an hour, trying to contact her with the crystal, then he'd been pacing his lair for two… and all he had to show for it was a headache.

And the ghost of her kiss still on his lips.

That kiss. If it weren't for that, he'd probably be in Seattle by now, swiping right on the WildLove app and looking to get laid quickly by whoever was available… *but that kiss.* It was hot—dragonfire hot—and yet fumbling and innocent and beautiful. Like her. She'd let go for the tiniest moment, and his heart had soared. It was just one kiss, but it was easily better than all his fantasies combined. There was no way he was letting go of that. And he didn't believe for a second that she couldn't love him. More than that… he was well convinced that she fled, twisting away through space and time with her angel magic, precisely because she was afraid.

Afraid she *could* love him.

He didn't understand why that frightened her so badly.

And he needed help figuring this out. Plus some plan to get her to accept his crystal-calls.

He checked the time on his phone—it was the middle of the day. So he quickly dialed Leonidas and hoped he wasn't waking the baby or something. As it rang, Leksander hustled out of his lair, heading for his brother's apartment. The keep was back to its normal daily operations, but the hallways were still empty.

Leonidas picked up. "Hey, my brother. How are you holding up?"

"I kissed Erelah." He felt foolish just blurting it out, like a young dragon before his first bedding. It was silly. And yet his heart trembled with it.

There was silence on the other end. Then, "You… did?"

"I need to talk to your mate." Rosalyn had been badgering him to confess his feelings. Well, now he had. And everything was in flames.

"Um… okay."

Leksander had reached their lair. "Good. I'm at your door." He hung up and knocked softly, just in case baby Thorn was sleeping.

It took a moment, but Rosalyn opened up. "Get straight out! You *kissed* her?"

Leksander grinned. "Yes."

She scowled. "What the hell are you doing at my door?"

His grin crumbled. "She vowed she could never love me and left."

Her expression softened. "Oh."

"Can I come in?"

"Yeah. Of course." She hustled back, opening the door wide. "Leonidas has the baby upstairs." She led him into the apartment and around the corner to the kitchen. "This sounds like a conversation that requires tea."

"What I need is your advice."

Rosalyn stopped and turned to face him, arms folded. "Okay. So, you kissed her. Did you tell her, you know, that you love her?"

"Not exactly."

She unlocked her arms in exasperation. "Oh, for the love of magic! *Leksander.*"

He held up his hands. "*I tried.* That's not where this went wrong."

She scowled and crossed her arms again. "I'm listening."

"She's convinced that she *can't* love me." He lifted his hands and shrugged because he wasn't sure about any of this. "Because she's angeling and somehow angelings can't love. Or at least *she* can't because she took some vow of chastity for her faction or some damn thing. I don't... is this just bullshit, Rosalyn? Is this what women say when what they really mean is *fuck you, go away, I hate you?* Because I can't figure this out, and she won't return my calls." The exasperation in his voice was making it hike up, so he stopped.

"Well, damn." She bit her lip. "But you *kissed* her. I mean... was it, you know, a weird kiss? It *has* been a while for you, dragon prince. Maybe it was just awkward?" She had a strange grimace, and it was making him uncomfortable just to watch.

"No." And he was emphatic about that. "The kiss was not the problem. Or maybe..." How to say this? "I think she's afraid of it. I think she's just... very new at the whole kissing thing."

Rosalyn raised her eyebrows. *"Oh.* Like she's never..." She vaguely gestured to Leksander.

"Never. Pretty certain about that." He grimaced. "But just being a virgin doesn't explain it either. It seems like... I don't know, like she's *afraid* of loving me. Only that doesn't make any sense."

Rosalyn rubbed her chin and looked thoughtful. "Maybe it's not so much loving you, but what it might cost her."

He frowned. "You think she's afraid of the mating?" He supposed that could be it. Erelah had been present at both births, and she knew the struggles of Rosalyn's pregnancy and Arabella's. He shook his head. "I can't really see that."

"No, I don't think that's it," Rosalyn agreed. "Erelah is a serious badass. So if she's *afraid*… it has to be something worse than dying. If that makes sense."

In a strange way, it did. "She said she would lay down her life for me. But that she couldn't love me."

"So let's say she did." Rosalyn shuffled over to the cupboard to pull out a mug. "Sorry, I need tea for this conversation. Baby-sleep-deprived."

Leksander took the cup from her and filled it with water then popped it in the microwave. Rosalyn rifled through another cupboard and came out with a tin of tea bags. They wafted a strong lemon scent through the air. She pulled out a foil bag and tapped the counter with it.

"So she falls in love with you," Rosalyn continued. "You make mad dragon love, you seal her with your mark, and she has a dragon-angel-baby with you. What happens then?"

Leksander couldn't help the small skip in his heart. Were they really talking about this like it was possible? Because he hadn't even let his own mind go there yet. "Then we live happily ever after?" Where was she going with this?

The microwave beeped, so he hurriedly extracted the cup and took the tea bag from her, carefully ripping the package and dunking the bag.

Rosalyn counted off on her fingers. "First, she's probably kicked out of the chastity club, am I right? How big of a deal is that for angelings?"

He frowned. "I don't know."

"Okay, so you need to find that out."

"All right."

She tapped another finger. "Second, can you even

make a baby with an angel? I mean, how does that work with your hot dragon-and-fae blood?"

"I don't know." His frown felt like it was carving into his face.

She scowled. "Has *anyone* crossed dragons and angels before?"

His heart was sinking. "Not to my knowledge."

"All right," she said with a sigh, like she couldn't believe he hadn't thought these things through. He was wondering himself. "So, maybe she gets kicked out of angel land. Maybe the baby isn't even viable. I guarantee she's got all this on her mind. Then third…" She tapped another finger. "Say you make the baby. Does it fulfill the treaty? Because you *know* she's all about the treaty."

"That's true." Dread was crowding in on his heart.

"So how do we know if this angeling-dragonling would fulfill the treaty?"

"I… I guess we would know when the baby was born," he said reluctantly. This wasn't good. "The treaty magic would renew. Everyone with immortal blood, bound by the treaty, would feel it."

"So… what if it doesn't work?" Rosalyn hiked her eyebrows up again. "You're going to run out and mate with someone else? Make a baby with a human?"

He grimaced. "You think all this is holding her back."

Rosalyn frowned, took the mug of tea from him, blew on it and took a sip. Finally, she said, "No, probably not."

Leksander's shoulders relaxed.

"It has to be something much worse than all that."

"Worse?" Okay, he was officially in over his head. "Rosalyn, I don't know what to do."

"You still love her, right?" She peered at him over the mug, sipping as the steam rose into her face.

"Yes." That much he knew.

"And this kiss… it was a *good* kiss, right?"

"Yes." He had to rein an explosion of fantasies crowding his mind. If a simple kiss with her had awoken every part of him so thoroughly, bringing new life to his heart most of all, what would making love be like? Much less sealing? His mind stalled out at mated sex because he was legitimately wondering if that was even possible now.

"Then, no matter what," Rosalyn said, nailing him with her brilliant blue eyes. "You go after that girl until you get her."

Relief washed through his body. "I don't know where to begin."

"You begin by finding out the answers to those questions," she said, nodding then sipping her tea again. "Because she's thought about all this, guaranteed. And something in there is scaring the crap out of a girl who's never even taken a man to bed, Leksander."

"You're right. Of course." He scowled, but it was for himself. How had he known Erelah for all these years and yet not know her mind at all? Or her life in the Dominion? It was as if he and Erelah had created their own little bubble where just the two of them existed. He knew that she loved flying through cool air the best, even better at night. He knew she preferred slaying demons on a full stomach, but she required little food because of her angel nature. But he had no idea she'd made this vow or what any of that meant.

Rosalyn was watching him, waiting.

He spread his hands wide. "She won't return my calls."

Her response was swift. "Then you find another way to reach her."

Leksander nodded.

A shuffle at the door to the kitchen drew their attention. Leonidas stood with a sleeping baby Thorn in his arms. He held out his other arm—his runes were in a frenzy. "We've got a problem."

Leksander scowled. "What's that?"

Rosalyn set down her mug and hurried over to take baby Thorn from her mate.

"Nyssa is coming to visit," Leonidas said grimly.

Leksander nearly choked. "What? When?"

"About five minutes. Come on." Leonidas was already heading out of the kitchen.

Leksander hurried after him, giving a grateful smile to Rosalyn on the way. Then he faced his brother as he slid open the door to his lair. "Why the hell is Nyssa coming here?"

"She didn't say," Leonidas said tightly. "But I got the sense she was pissed."

Leksander swallowed. "Do we have some kind of weapons we can use against the fae? If it comes to that?"

Leonidas shook his head. "Just the wards. Which is why we're meeting her in the throne room and, under no circumstances are we dropping the wards on the rest of the keep." He gave Leksander a sideways look. "Do you want to sit this out? She won't be able to get to you through the wards."

Leksander scoffed. "I'm not hiding while my brothers take on the Queen of the Summer Court."

Leonidas smirked. "Oh, no, it'll just be me. Lucian's the king—I'm not even telling him until she's gone—and the young princes stay safely behind the wards. And I'm not too excited about you being there, even though she insisted. I'm not letting Nyssa take down our chance to renew the treaty. I know she can't kill you outright, my brother—"

Leksander gave him a skeptical look as they strode through the corridor. "Are you sure about that?"

Leonidas drew away from him. "Yes?"

"She *is* summer fae." Leksander frowned.

Leonidas shook his head. "No, that doesn't matter. Remember, the original treaty was protecting the queen's bastard child from her king. And her previous children. Nyssa was one of those, right? She's absolutely bound by the treaty. If not, the House of Smoke would have been dead ten thousand years ago."

Leksander nodded. That made sense. It also reminded him that Nyssa was really fucking old, even though her beauty was eternal. "Then let me handle this. It's me she's angry with."

"Be my guest." Leonidas pulled open the door to the throne room and gestured him inside. "Just don't get yourself dead, okay? You've got business left to attend to."

Leksander nodded and strode into the throne room. He was surprised to see half the House had hastily assembled. How Leonidas managed to keep Lucian in the dark, he had no idea, but his brother would probably pay for that later. Cinaed was up front, and he probably had something to do with it. Strangely, Rachel was by his side, arguing with him. Their whispers ceased as soon as Leksander was within earshot.

Leksander tipped his head to Cinaed. "You needn't bring your mate to this," he said, then winced because he'd forgotten that they hadn't yet mated.

"Tell him *he* doesn't need to be here either," Rachel shot back.

Cinaed glared at her. "My place is defending the House and its prince."

Leksander raised his eyebrows and glanced at Leonidas, but he just shook his head. To Cinaed, Leksander said, "You needn't be here, Cinaed. This is my screw-up to fix."

"No, my liege," Cinaed said, holding his head high. "Your House stands with you."

All the House's dragons combined would be nothing against the fae queen if she arrived deciding to wreak vengeance. The treaty protected the royalty of the House of Smoke, but not its members.

Leksander swung back to Leonidas, who had taken a stance in front of the throne chairs. "Maybe we shouldn't have assembled half the House here."

His brother grimaced. "The queen requested it."

Oh fuck. That wasn't good. "Still, let's send back—" The air popped, cutting him off, and a hush fell over the whispering crowd of dragons that filled half the hall.

Leksander's attention—along with everyone else's—was drawn to the center of the room where Nyssa had suddenly appeared. This time she wore black, only it was a kind of erotic battle armor. A high-collared vest was cut away at the bottom, baring skin from the under curve of her breasts down to below her navel. The black, sheer skirt she wore low on her hips was cut into four sections with more leg showing than covered. Her high-heeled, black boots covered the most skin of anything, stretching halfway up her thighs.

It was an outfit for adventures in the bedroom, and by the furious look in her violet eyes as she sauntered forward, she was on the hunt for someone to drag back there. But as she strolled past the assembled dragons she asked for, she only had eyes for him.

"Nyssa," Leksander said carefully in greeting. "Didn't expect to see you so soon."

She gave an elaborate pout. "You injured my pride, dragon prince. I had to console myself for a while."

Leksander lifted one eyebrow. He could easily imagine Kalen was involved in this *consoling.* But now that she was back, what did that mean? "I meant no offense, Nyssa. It was… a slip of the tongue." His stomach tightened. The last thing he wanted was a return trip to Nyssa's bedchambers. He had finally had a breakthrough with Erelah—that needed all his attention.

She stepped up on the dais, just one step below where he and Leonidas stood. Her smile was dripping with lascivious intent. "Perhaps I was hasty in throwing you out of my bed."

Leksander grimaced and tried to ignore the whisperings that ran through the hall. He hadn't exactly announced his intent to seduce the queen. "Perhaps I was hasty to offer to fill it."

That was obviously the wrong thing to say. Nyssa's seductive smile quickly twisted into anger. "Then I shall have one of your men instead. And perhaps I shall decide to *keep* him."

Leksander swallowed. "Nyssa, as we agreed before, volunteers only—"

"Are *you* volunteering?" There was a flash of pain in her eyes, but it was quickly banished as she stepped up to stand directly in front of him, only inches between them now. He steeled himself not to back away. She dropped her voice, a whisper just for him, although the throne room had hushed to listen, including Leonidas who stood next to him, looking horrified but staying silent. "Because for *you*, I can be forgiving," she said. "*You* came to *me*, dragon prince. And your offer was… *enticing.* All will be forgotten if you return. We will make a love that will be storied for its strength and power. But *deny me*… and I shall fill my needs in other ways."

Leksander gritted his teeth. "Nyssa, you don't want—"

She leaned in fast, stopping just before her lips might

reach his. "But I *do* want, dragon prince," she whispered, voice breathless with promise. "Do not deny me."

But he had to. "Don't do this, Nyssa."

The anger settled, terrifying and cold and fast in her violet eyes. She stepped back. "Very well." Then she whirled to face the assembly of dragons.

What was he doing? Sacrificing one of his dragons, just so he could pursue Erelah? Who may not even be capable of loving him? The dishonor of that was rumbling around deep inside him, but it stepped up to alarm when Nyssa strutted straight over to Cinaed.

"This one," she proclaimed. Then she put a hand to his cheek, and Cinaed fell to his knees, eyes closed, mouth open and instantly panting.

"No!" Rachel cried out by his side. She lunged at the queen's arm. The dragons closest to her couldn't stop her before the queen flicked a finger and sent Rachel sailing through the air. One of the dragons caught her, breaking her fall.

"*Nyssa!*" Leksander roared. He leaped off the dais and stomped to her side. "Release him!"

She didn't, just turned to Leksander, her eyes hooded with the pleasure she and Cinaed were sharing. "You know what I want," she breathed.

"Release him," Leksander said again, only this time he used the dominating voice he'd brought to their little power play in her bedroom.

Her eyes flashed, and Cinaed slumped away from her touch. She turned to face Leksander, eyes sparkling with anticipation.

"Return to your Court," he said in the same commanding tone. "I have things to attend to here. I will arrive in a week's time. Prepare yourself for me." *Holy magic,* he hoped he could find a way out of this by then.

Her lips twitched like she was repressing a smile. "Two days, my prince. I'll be ready." The smile broke through, eager and hungry, just as she stepped back and twisted to disappear.

Leksander let out the breath he'd been holding.

Leonidas appeared by his side. Rachel had found her way to helping Cinaed up from the ground. The young blue dragon looked tormented.

"My liege," he croaked. "What deal have you struck?"

"One hopefully I won't have to keep." Leksander couldn't help his grimace, though. This left him almost no time to sort things out with Erelah.

"What *is* your intention here, my brother?" Leonidas asked, eyebrows raised.

"To obtain a mate," Leksander ground out. "One way or another." Then he lifted his chin to Cinaed and gave a pointed look to Rachel. "Something you should consider as well."

Cinaed's eyes were still wide from his encounter with the queen, but he turned to Rachel and took her hands in his. "My love…"

"It's okay," she said quickly. "I know you wouldn't have, well… wanted to. Or enjoyed it. Not much, anyway. With the queen, I mean."

Cinaed was shaking his head and smiling. "Will you stop making my excuses, please?"

"I'm just saying—" She cut off as Cinaed dropped to one knee.

"Rachel, my love," he said. "I've wanted so long to say…" He seemed to choke up. "I feared the risk. The sealing fraught with danger. The child who might not live. All of it struck a terror in my heart that froze me cold. But I can't take the chance that…" He hesitated again.

Rachel's eyes were filling with tears.

"Tomorrow is not promised," Cinaed choked out. "All we may have is today. And if that's all there is to be mine, I want it all with you. Will you do me the honor of becoming my mate?"

"Oh my god, yes!" She threw her arms around Cinaed's neck, and he pulled her to the floor with him, kissing her soundly. A whoop of approval and applause went up around the throne room, and there were smiles all around.

Even Leksander had one wrenched onto his face.

It was about time for the two of them. And far beyond time for him and Erelah. Cinaed had it precisely right— tomorrow was *not* promised. Even more so for the last unmated prince of the House of Smoke. Leksander needed to convince his beloved angeling that love could overcome any obstacle, including whatever immutable thing she thought stood in their way. And that love was worth fighting for.

Cinaed whisked Rachel off her feet and was carrying her from the throne room to thunderous applause.

As Leksander watched them go, Leonidas spoke softly to him, "Two days, Leksander. And what do we do then?"

"I'm leaving that to you, my brother. I have a mate to seduce." By which he meant Erelah, and Leonidas's slow nod said he understood. Leksander clapped him on the back and strode after Cinaed and his soon-to-be mate.

If only Leksander could be so lucky.

Chapter Eleven

"So the dragon prince still has love of you?"

Markos's voice rang clear through the gathering room. The angelings met here when not engaged in training or seclusion or sleep. Erelah stood at the far end in the alcove where Markos received petitions and reports, but it was not meant for privacy. There were no private places except one's own cloister cell, and even there, it was meant more to minimize distraction, not keep secrets. All things were known to all the company of angelkind.

Including her shame.

The other angelings of her faction were hushed; too hushed. Listening to every word.

"I told him it was impossible," Erelah said. "And I left quickly." She hadn't told yet of the kiss because her heart panicked each time she thought of it.

"After he healed you." Markos's voice was cool, measured. But it was always like that. The True Angels were exquisite in the Virtue of Patience.

"Yes." Erelah dropped her head. "My blood is now mixed. Dragon and…" She lowered her voice even though it was pointless. "…and fae." Was it her imagination that the hall had gone even more quiet?

The amount of fae magic within her was minuscule. And she suspected her angel nature had already snuffed it out, for she hardly felt it.

"Yes, I noticed as soon as you returned," Markos said.

Or maybe not. Erelah's shoulders drooped. "He was only trying to heal me. I was in torment yet with the shadow strike and…" She looked up and tried to regain some of her dignity. "It was a Kindness. Not to allow it would have been uncharitable." It was a decent explanation and a partial truth. When she searched her heart, she knew she simply couldn't refuse him, not when the torment on his face was so plain. And the shadow strike had made her very sick. She hadn't the will to refuse him in that state. Besides, it would have taken her a long time to recover without his assistance… but those were excuses. *Truth.* She was trying to adhere to it as much as possible. The truth was that she welcomed Leksander's offer to heal her because she *desired* it.

Which was part of why she needed to seek Penance.

Markos was carefully examining her. His angel nature let him see into her soul in ways she couldn't even understand. No doubt he saw her guilt, hanging over it like a plague, even if he didn't know the exact reason.

"It's imperative that the prince finds a mate," Markos said, finally.

"I understand," Erelah said quickly. "Which is why I seek a transfer and some time in Penance." The Penance was for *her.* She needed to purge the guilt of that kiss— guilt for leading Leksander on, for never seeing his love before now, for subjecting him to years of torment in unrequited love. But the *transfer* was for Leksander's sake —to take her irrevocably away from him, so she would risk no more harm. And to convince him to move on quickly.

For it was Tajael's words which haunted her the most. *He would never let you go.*

All the Angels in Heaven, please don't let that be true.

"A transfer will not fix this, Erelah." There was too much Kindness in his voice! Her heart spasmed. He was going to turn her down.

"If you would recommend me to apprentice," she pleaded, "in the Diligence Faction, I hear tell that their apprenticeship includes a seclusion. It cannot be reversed once started. The prince would be forced to seek a mate elsewhere. I am already refusing his summons. Once I am apprenticed, word could be sent that I have gone into an irreversible retreat. A decade would suffice. Enough that he would know the impossibility of the situation."

He coolly regarded her. "And your Penance?"

She nodded quickly. "I was thinking the Worship Choir. Not all ten years, perhaps. But as long as I'm able." Worship was arduous but among the most purifying of Penance duties. Perpetual angelsong, given in worship to God. Every waking hour was spent in that state, nearly pulled apart at the seams by not only your own song but the resonance with the others. It was really the province of the Angels, but the angelings had their own choir. Most lasted only a few months. Others became inured in a way and stayed until they withered to nothing. It was how some angelings gave their lives, singing praise until the very end. It was a noble and righteous way to die, if that were necessary.

She didn't want to die. But if that were required to free the prince from her, then she would make that sacrifice. It was as she told him—she would readily lay down her life for his. And she knew Markos would understand. If he suggested a lengthy Penance in Choir, she knew what that meant. And she would accept it.

But he was taking too long to consider her request.

She waited, counting this as work on her least favorite Virtue. *Patience.*

Finally, Markos said, "I don't think it's wise for you to leave Chastity at this time, Erelah."

Her shoulders sagged again. "But I could——"

He raised a finger, so she shut her mouth. "You're to remain available to Tajael while the situation in the House of Smoke is waiting to resolve. You are still our best source of understanding about the ways of the dragons, and your contribution there may yet be required."

A panicky despair gripped her heart. "May I not have even a small Penance?" She wasn't sure how she could endure this. She needed to do *something.* Seclusion in her room would drive her mad.

Markos gave her a look filled with Kindness. "Reconciliation with Tajael is where you should start."

Angels of light... that was the thing she least wanted to do. Which probably made it the most righteous Penance. She nodded dully. Markos dismissed her with a wave. She dragged her wings through the gathering room, stares following her the entire way.

No transfer.

No Penance.

Somehow she had to ignore Leksander's insistent calls *and* make peace with Tajael. She avoided her cell, as the crystal she gave to Leksander was taken from the walls of her room. When he spoke to it, the walls whispered in his voice. She *couldn't* be there, not knowing when he might try again. So she wandered the Dominion, ostensibly searching for Tajael. He wasn't in his cell or the gathering room she just left nor the training room. Finally, she asked after him and heard told he was hunting demons in Seattle. *Of course.* Carrying on with Diligence, that was Tajael.

She changed out of her still blood-soaked clothes into something fresh and appropriate for hunting—a snug halter top and wrapped leggings. They suited better for flying through the human realm, even if they looked more Warrior class than Protector. Mercifully, Leksander didn't call during the brief time she was in her room. She twisted her angel magic and popped out over Seattle.

The night sky was clouded, but the buildings below glittered.

She unfurled her wings and soared, relishing the cool night air and the way it washed her body clean. It didn't take long to find Tajael—his angel essence was unmistakable in a city drenched in human, shifter, and witch scents, along with an abundance of demon. No wonder Tajael was busy here. He ought to recruit a legion of angelings to assist him, but that decision befell Markos, and for whatever reason, he was holding back. Perhaps not wanting to provoke the fae, although Erelah could see no sense in that.

She flew over the alleyway where she sensed Tajael just as he soared up and out, carrying an elderly woman. He alit on the rooftop with his rescued human, deftly cleaving the demon and breathing life into her. Erelah landed nearby and waited for him to finish. The woman toddled off, a fresh lift to her step when he was done, and Tajael's cheeks were rosy with the aftereffects of the life kiss he'd bestowed.

"You're back!" Tajael said, all smiles and flushed happiness. "And in good health I see." Then he frowned.

"And carrying Leksander's blood," Erelah added. There was no sense in avoiding the topic. It was plain for Tajael to sense. Any angel worth their wings could detect their avowed enemy. Erelah was more used to it than the others, with all the time she spent with Leksander.

Even that brief thought of him made the broken-wide rift inside her ache a little more.

"Well, then," Tajael said, seeming nonplussed. "That is an interesting turn."

"I… he, um…" It was at the tip of her mouth, the words about the kiss.

"He healed you," Tajael offered with a small frown, as if confused why she couldn't speak it.

"He kissed me." There, a confession.

Tajael's eyebrows flew up, and he leaned back. "Oh."

"I wanted to pay my Penance in the Worship Choir," she said, "but Markos made me come say I'm sorry to you instead."

A smile grew slowly across Tajael's face, then he finally burst out with a short laugh.

"It's not funny." She scowled at him.

He was still grinning. "I've forgiven you, E. Don't you see?"

She frowned. "No."

"And Markos knows it."

She scowled. "That doesn't make any sense."

His smile faded a little, and he frowned as well. "No, it doesn't. But you know how Angels are. Or rather, they're impossible to understand. But Markos must have some other intent, sending you here rather than locking you away in Worship."

Erelah gave her head a small shake. She'd felt *off* since Leksander's healing, but she figured it was just the trauma of the kiss. Now she wondered if the fae and dragon magic were still warring with her angel nature or some such thing. Making it difficult to focus.

Either way, her mind was too tormented to follow

where Tajael was leading. "What is Markos's intent with this?"

He spread his hands wide then his wings. "Who knows?" He wasn't flying just flexing them and shaking off the effects of the life kiss. "By all that's holy, Erelah, I would tell you. Let's just say the Angels are mysterious, and we know not always their ways." He grimaced. "Shall we hunt demon? I'm getting rather addicted to this line of work."

She shook her head at him. "Then you should stop."

"Probably." He smirked in that rascally way of his. "But not quite yet." He flexed his wings and lifted off from the roof.

She leaped into the air to follow, but just as her feet left the rooftop, something slammed hard into her back and down she went, skittering across the rough tar-paper roof. She reflexively sprung up and pulsed power away from her, but then Tajael fell from the sky, missing the edge of the building and plummeting seven stories below.

"Tajael!" She leaped into the air again, but something snared her and fouled her wings and dragged her back to the rooftop. This time she twisted around to see a man standing not ten feet from her—no, not a man. *Fae.*

He had fiery red hair, pointed ears, and a web of golden energy he had thrown over her. It burned like fire-brands wherever it touched, and he reeled her in like fish caught in a net. The golden lines pulsed as she fought them, and she only became more entangled the more she struggled. The fae advanced on her. She rose up on magic alone, dragging him with her along the rooftop, but he stayed on his feet, and with the hand not gripped on her golden energy leash, he sent a pulse of energy that knocked her from the sky again. She hit hard, and it dazed her. She tried twisting time and space—an escape back to her Dominion—but the golden netting was blocking any use of magic. Before she could move again, he was upon her, his cold hand reaching through the netting to her bare flesh.

An instant later, the familiar folding of space and time told her he was taking her somewhere.

She was caught.

Chapter Twelve

Two days to convince Erelah to love him, and she wasn't even taking his calls.

What the hell was he doing?

He'd just tried the crystal again, but it was no use. He was getting desperate enough to call on Markos, but he didn't know how—it wasn't like the House of Smoke had ever contacted the Angels *on purpose*. And now that he was cut off, Leksander felt the hopelessness of the situation even more strongly.

How could he be in love with Erelah all these years and not really understand who she was? Or what was causing her to run so far and so fast from him? He was pursuing her, but did he even know her? He was afraid the answer to that was obvious. *No*. And if he didn't understand her, there was no hope of wooing her.

He was perched at the calling station for the keep—a tiny, rocky ledge just outside the perimeter alarms. The keep was locked down again with extra wards, so any immortal creature who wanted to call must stop here first and make contact. Ostensibly, he was here in case Erelah decided to show up, but in actuality, he was going crazy cooped up in his lair, pacing while he tried to sort all this out. He'd given up on the crystal, and it was a struggle not to give up on his angeling altogether.

His angeling. When did he start to think of her as belonging to him? She was fierce and proud and strong—Erelah would never *belong* to anyone, not in the sense of being owned or kept or controlled. It was one of the things that intrigued him about her. The raw energy and vibrancy and *goodness* of her was a constant draw for him, always bringing him back, even when he was frustrated or hopeless that they would ever have more than friendship. Was it really not meant to be? Could an angeling as pure of heart as Erelah only ever belong to her faction? Maybe that was why she was afraid. She feared that her friendship with him might slide into something more intimate—that kiss was enough to set him on fire; if it did the same to her, that would be cause for alarm. Especially if it broke her vow and would get her kicked out of her Dominion. If *that* was where she was meant to be, he could understand why she would run from *him*. And what kind of selfish bastard was he to screw that up for her?

Fuck. A roar welled up from inside him, sudden and hot. He shifted to dragon and raked his claws into the rocky ledge as he bellowed out his anger in a screech and in dragonfire. The echo bounced off the keep and the distant rock faces of the mountains. Then he sagged down on his haunches, defeated. He had a glimmer of the agony his brothers must have felt when they believed their mates were hopelessly out of reach. And while his disposition would never let him drop into those depths of despair, his situation was probably the most impossible of the three.

The air next to him compressed and then made a small popping sound—the kind that proceeded Erelah whenever she appeared at his side. His heart leaped as he twisted his long, dragon neck to see… but it was only Tajael.

Fucking Tajael. The last person he wanted to see.

"Oh!" Tajael said, stepping back in surprise. "I guess you really *are* a dragon."

Leksander snarled, then quickly shifted human to speak. "What do you want?" Only then did Leksander notice the charred burns across Tajael's toga. "And what happened to you?"

The surprise on Tajael's face was quickly replaced with concern. "It's what's happened to Erelah that matters."

"What?" Leksander turned to fully face him. "What are you talking about?"

"She's been taken." Tajael's voice was edged with panic. "By the fae."

"The fae?" Leksander's voice hiked up. Panic gripped his chest. "How…? *When?"*

"I'm not sure," Tajael said with a grimace. "I was knocked out. I just barely glimpsed the man who took her, but I'm certain he was fae. I could sense his power. He appeared next to Erelah and attacked. She was on a rooftop in Seattle. We were to go demon hunting. I was already lifted above, taken unawares, just as she was." There was an apology in his voice, and guilt and concern, but Leksander didn't care about any of that.

"Are you *certain* he was fae?" Although who else could take an angeling by surprise, much less kidnap one?

"Yes. Mostly." Tajael pressed his lips together. "It happened fast."

"It could be Zephan," Leksander said. And how truly fucked was he, if that were true? "He's come after each of my brothers and their mates. Maybe he realized that… that I have feelings for her…" He stalled out and drew back from Tajael.

The angeling gave him an exasperated look. "I know your thoughts on this," he said impatiently. "The entire realm does. Not least because I told them."

Leksander squinted. That grated against his nerves, which were raw as it was, but he needed to stay focused. If Erelah was taken by Zephan… "But why now?" Leksander asked. Maybe he had this all wrong, and he didn't want to go running down the wrong path because he was panicked and not thinking clearly. "Zephan has to have known of my love for Erelah long before now." Then he remembered that Zephan came hunting after Leonidas and Rosalyn when her love became True. That was the signal. That was the treaty defining act that reverberated across magical space… and drew Zephan to them like a spider on its web. *Could Erelah love him?* The idea seized him so hard he couldn't speak for a moment.

"I don't know why—" Tajael was saying.

"Did she say something," Leksander interrupted. "Something that made you think that she… that her feelings for me might have, well, changed?" He couldn't help the hope in his voice.

But Tajael's expression seemed pained. "I don't think that's it, Leksander."

A vise squeezed tighter on his chest, but more than disappointment, he was angry with himself. He was worried whether she loved him? When she was potentially in mortal danger?

He shook his head. "That doesn't matter—"

"No, it does," Tajael said, gravely. "A great deal. But I didn't come here to torment you, prince of the House of Smoke. No matter Erelah's feelings in the matter, your affection for her makes her a threat to anyone who wishes for the treaty to fall."

"Zephan." His name was ash in Leksander's mouth.

Never mind that Zephan's powers were greater than any dragon, even one with fae blood. If he hurt Erelah, Leksander would make him pay. In blood.

"I fear so," Tajael said. "But I can't take this to Markos. He may just allow the fae to have her."

"*What?*"

Tajael grimaced again. "You have to understand—I cannot make war between fae and angelkind. The taking of an angeling is a direct provocation, but preserving the treaty—keeping the fae from interfering with humanity—is far more important. Markos knows you love Erelah, which is also a direct threat to the treaty. With her removed from the situation…"

"He would just sacrifice her?" Leksander's mouth went dry. Damn these Angels and their self-sacrificial righteousness!

"He would if it served the greater needs of humanity. Yes." There was no room for doubt in his voice, and Leksander wouldn't have questioned it anyway.

It just horrified him. "Well, fuck him."

Tajael choked out what seemed like a small laugh. "Yes. So to speak. Which is why I came to you, prince of the House of Smoke. I know you have love of her—don't hold it against her if she cannot return that same feeling to you."

Leksander winced, but there was no question in his mind of whether he would go after her. The only question was *how*. "It doesn't matter if she loves me—"

"I know that it does," Tajael said, but it was gentle. Kind-hearted. The same kind of voice Erelah often used with him. It made his heart ache. "You have to understand that angelings aren't raised how humans, or even princes of the House of Smoke, are brought up. We're taken from our human mothers almost the moment we're born. We raised in the Dominion. The first time we even have a chance to encounter humanity is on our coming of age, during our walkabout. That's when many Fall and are lost."

"You mean they sleep with humans." This was the essence of it—Erelah was terrified even of a kiss because she thought it might lead to more.

"It's more than that... but yes." Tajael's eyes narrowed. "You have to understand, prince of the House of Smoke. No one has ever loved Erelah. Not a mother. Not a lover. There is only the pure love that an Angel can bring, and let me assure you, it is *not* the same."

Leksander blinked and drew back. "But I've loved her—"

"She has not known of it," Tajael said, gently. "And that makes all the difference. I remember the first time a human had love of me... I almost didn't survive it. The pull was so great, the temptation so strong..." He swallowed. "Know that this is what Erelah is facing. She has never had what you offer with a clear and open heart, and yet, if she partakes, it will be her downfall."

"Why?" Leksander demanded, suddenly seizing on this. Because this had to be the key. "Is it her vow of Chastity? Can that never be broken?"

"It's more than that." Tajael grimaced. "The vow keeps her safe."

Leksander frowned. "I don't understand."

Tajael shook his head. "The vow is no burden to me— I would never be tempted to bring a child into this world, not knowing the burden every angeling has to carry. The walkabout serves that very purpose—to go out in the world and know its temptations then return to take the vow when one is ready. Erelah returned almost immediately, but in a way, she has never returned."

Leksander gave him a pinched look. This angeling was talking in circles.

Tajael gestured to him. "She has been your friend from the beginning, yes? It's as though she never left the human realm, not truly. She found a human, albeit one with dragon and fae blood, who offered something also scarce in the Dominion—true friendship. She's held onto that even as she took her vow. And Markos allowed it because she *didn't* love you. But don't hold that against her, Leksander. It's literally the only thing that allows her to continue."

"I told you, it doesn't matter to me if Erelah loves me or not." At Tajael's skeptical look, he quickly added. *"Of course,* I wish she loved me. I want her to *need* me like I need air to breathe. What I mean is that none of that will stop me from killing any fae who might harm her."

The tension in Tajael's body relaxed. "A True Love then," he said, approvingly. "I cannot implore the Winter Court to return her or release her, but you can, prince of the House of Smoke. Your True Love gives you cause."

Leksander nodded, seeing where he was going with this. Finally. "I'll demand her return under the terms of the treaty—that it protects the future potential mates of the House of Smoke. If I truly love her, then that has to put the protection over her, even if she's an angeling. Even if she doesn't yet love *me.*"

"I'm not sure if that will be true, magically speaking," he said, gravely. "But she *is* half human. It might be a convincing argument, regardless."

Leksander nodded. The two were standing face to face on the narrow rocky ledge—it was the perfect place to summon Zephan. "I can call the Winter Court. Demand that Zephan account for what's happened."

Tajael nodded, stepping back to the far edge of the

outcropping and drawing his blade from a sheath at his hip. "I cannot travel to the fae domain without being at the mercy of the Court. But here, in this realm? I'll have your back, prince of the House of Smoke."

Leksander was less concerned for himself—he was protected by the treaty—but having an angeling on hand might help convince Zephan to give Erelah over. Leksander clasped his hands together, summoning his inner fae magic. The runes skittered down his arms, pooling where this fingers had hold of one another, and he reached into that magic space where the fae lived. He couldn't travel as they did—his magic wasn't strong enough—but just like he summoned the Queen of the Summer Court, he could tap on the door of the Winter Court. He focused on Zephan in particular, imagining his long, dark hair, cruel icy blue eyes, and that smirk. It wasn't hard to imagine a thousand talon strikes drawing his blood but then again, maybe that was exactly the message he wanted to send.

It took a long time—a full minute of seconds ticking by —but Zephan finally popped out of the fae realm and onto the rocky ledge in front of Leksander.

"Enough of your fantasies, dragon-beast!" Zephan snarled.

That drew an instant smile to Leksander's face. He had no idea he could get under Zephan's skin so easily. Then he killed the smile in favor of a blood-letting glare and a shifting to talons for both hands. *Return my mate,* he snarled.

Zephan drew back, wary, flicking a look at Tajael. "What in magic are you—"

"One of your minions has taken Erelah, the angeling I intend as my mate." The growl was working its way out of his chest. "Return her. *Now,* Zephan. Or you're going to really wish you had." He wasn't sure he could back up that threat, but he would find a way.

Zephan gave him an odd pinched look, like he couldn't decide if Leksander was joking or not. Which just inflamed Leksander more—was this nothing but games to the vile fae prince? But then a more familiar disdain took over Zephan's face.

"If someone of my Court had taken your little bird, trust me, I would know it." He drew himself up to his full, haughty height. "You're growling up the wrong Court, dragon-beast." Then he turned and disappeared into a flash of light.

Leksander just gaped at the empty space where Zephan was a moment ago... and a realization sunk down on his chest, squeezing it even harder.

"He's lying," Tajael offered. "The fae always lie, even though, in theory, they cannot."

Leksander turned to face him, the full horror of this making it hard for him to breathe. "He's not lying. And I know who has her."

"Who?" Tajael had an almost comical look of confusion on his face.

"Nyssa. Queen of the Summer Court." Leksander's throat closed up.

Erelah... what had he done?

Chapter Thirteen

relentless.

Erelah bashed against the golden bars that held her like a giant caged bird, but everywhere she touched—the bars, the golden floor, the domed top—*burned* with an unholy fire. Already her wings and arms and feet bore a hundred scorch marks. Only by lifting on magic alone, keeping her wings tucked, could she avoid contact with the sizzling evil magic of the cage, which dangled from the ceiling. But she could only do that for so long before she tired… and scorched her feet once more.

"You fae are even more loathsome than I knew," Erelah spat at the male fae who was cooling watching her struggles. She was suspended in the middle of a room that seemed more like a forest. Vines hung from the ceiling, partially blocking Erelah's view of an elaborate twist of roots and flowers in the shape of a throne. In the middle of it was a swing.

The Summer Court. She was sure of it. Not only the wild nature of the place, but she tasted the summer magic on the fae before her. It was just like Leksander's. Not that the knowledge helped her in the slightest.

Erelah banged against the bars, this time unintentionally—her wings had flexed under the strain of staying aloft.

"Don't burn yourself to a crisp before the queen arrives," said the male fae who was her guard and jailer. "That takes all the fun out of it."

Erelah glared at him, but her heart was quivering more than her lungs. *The queen?* Why had she snatched Erelah off a rooftop in Seattle? And would Markos come for her? Somehow, she doubted it. And poor Tajael...

"The angeling you struck from the air..." Erelah paused. Would they tell her the truth? Supposedly, the fae *must* tell the truth, but in reality, they were artful about their lies. "Did you strike him with a lethal blow?" she asked. Perhaps that would pin him down sufficiently.

The fae looked annoyed, scowling at her with those green eyes as if he wished not to answer her at all, but finally, he blurted out, "No."

"So Tajael lives?" She bobbed in her cage, relaxing the constant effort at magic just for a second.

"How should I know?" The fae waved away her question. "It is unimportant."

"Because you were after me." Although she had yet to understand *why*.

An evil smirk slowly grew on his face. "Yes."

"What need have you of an angeling in a cage?" Her voice hiked up. The bloodlust and other cruelties of the fae were legion among the angelings of her Dominion. That a captured angeling might be abused for sport was not unheard of. After all, she would happily fling her blade and impale this vile creature, but he'd quickly disarmed her.

She could expect substantially worse than a quick death in return.

Angel and fae were ancient and mortal enemies.

There was little hope of escape.

"My queen will soon decide just what we'll do with you." He took pleasure in those words, and Erelah struggled not to lose heart. But what tiny hope she had was squashed when another fae winked into existence beside the first… only this one was female, with abundant white-silver hair, a vaporous dress made of the same silver-and-white coloration, and the pointed ears for which all fae were known.

The queen. It could be none other.

Her violet eyes were pale and angry, and she slowly circled Erelah in her cage, examining her. Erelah twisted to turn, continuing to face the queen in her inspection. Irritation flashed across the queen's face, and Erelah felt a flicker of satisfaction at having foiled her.

But it was short-lived.

The queen swept her hand around in a wave, and Erelah's cage suddenly tipped sideways, then upside down, then quickly right again. But she bashed against the bars with her wings and hands, the sizzling burn making her grunt deep in her throat while she clenched her teeth against the scream. Once upright again, she could keep afloat with magic and away from the bars, but the cruel smirk on the queen's face said she'd made her point.

She could hurt Erelah.

Only Erelah had no understanding of *why*. That the fae were evil by nature was given. But even evil had purpose behind it. Or did they simply take pleasure from torturing other beings? Disturbingly, that was possible.

Erelah shuddered but held as still as she could. This was not the glorious ending she had envisioned for her

Penance, but submitting to this torture could suffice. If the charring of her feathers and her flesh helped her pay for her Sins, then it would be a true Penance. Surely even Markos would agree with that. And she couldn't help thinking there was poetry in this, a capture and torture by the summer fae, the very bloodline to which Leksander belonged, and whom she had wronged through her inaction and tormented through her actions.

The shaking of her wings stilled, and she faced this Penance as she should—with acceptance and welcoming for its absolution.

"So you are Erelah," the queen said, raking her gaze over Erelah's floating body.

"Yes." How did the queen know her?

"I don't see the attraction."

What? Erelah just frowned and watched as the queen circled the cage. This time, Erelah closed her eyes and tipped her head back, letting the queen have her inspection as she waited for the strikes against her body. The shuffle of the queen's feet along the grass reached Erelah's ears, but the cage remained still, as far as she could tell with her eyes closed.

"What does Leksander see in you?"

Erelah popped open her eyes and looked down.

The queen's violet gaze locked with hers.

Erelah waited a heartbeat, then two. What had this to do with Leksander? "I don't know what you…" She stalled out at the queen's look of disgust.

The queen waved a hand, and Erelah's cage was cut loose. It crashed to the grass below, landing with a jarring *thunk* that threw Erelah against the magical burning of the floor. She screeched this time—it was out before she could stop it—then she flung herself up by reflex, panting and grimacing with the pain, but keeping aloft, away from the bars and the roof and the floor.

The red-headed male fae stood behind the queen, a smirk on his face. The air smelled of her own burnt feathers mixed in with the fresh scent of the grass, the vines, and the flowers that carpeted the floor and the walls. The queen stalked up to the cage, only a foot away, and glared at Erelah. Even though she floated, Erelah was at the same height as the tall queen, only her feet were tucked up, knees crooked to the side, to avoid the floor.

"He says you do not love him," the queen said, her gaze intense on Erelah's face. "Is this true?"

Was it true? "I have love of him as a friend," she said, resolutely. And she supposed it was true. What did she know about loving any other way? And only Tajael and Leksander could even rightly be called her friends. All others in her faction were friendly, but they had not the bond of years and demon slaying and trials they shared together. Even in that, Leksander stood alone, for had she not helped with the birthing of his nephews? Were they not in common cause to renew the treaty? He was unique in all she knew.

The queen's disgust was back. "A friend."

"Yes." Erelah wondered if that would occasion more torture. She almost hoped it would, rather than continue this torture-by-words.

The queen raised her hand. "I should kill you." She said it softly as if speaking to herself.

Erelah braced herself for the blow. If the queen simply ended it, that would be Penance enough.

"Why don't you plead for your life?" the queen suddenly shrieked, the power of her voice booming. It wasn't angelsong, but an echo of what that could be.

Erelah jolted from the shock but said nothing.

The queen turned to the male fae behind her. "Leave us." She waved him away. He snarled then disappeared. The queen stepped closer to Erelah's cage. "Is it the wings? It can't be your beauty," she said, disdainfully. "You wear it like armor."

Erelah just stared at her, confused. That sounded strangely like a compliment, but she knew that wasn't possible.

The queen leaned even closer and hissed, "Is it because he *cannot* have you? Is that it? All this pristine love-liness just out of *reach.*" And with the last word, the queen shoved back, and Erelah's cage went tumbling across the grass, crashing through vines, battering her with rapid-fire burns across her wings and back and hands as she braced against the worst of it. Then she crashed to a stop, and the side of her face momentarily was flung against the bars. She screamed again then jerked back, forcing herself to magick away from the walls of the cage, which was now canted to one side, propped up against a throne chair made of roots. The sizzling of the bars didn't seem to harm the chair, but each contact sapped Erelah of more angel power. She needed to rest. Recharge. Normally, Penance would take you to your limits, let you rest, then come back for more. *This…* much more of this, and she truly might not survive it. Not once she lost the ability to remain aloft.

She curled up, wings tucked, eyes closed, keeping as far from the walls as possible.

Even so, she listed to the side a little, struggling.

A tromping of feet through the grass announced the queen was back at her side. When Erelah opened her eyes, she saw the queen had bent down to peer at her. "He doesn't need the likes of you," she hissed.

Erelah just nodded. What could she say? Her mind was

tiring, dulled by the pain, but this wasn't idle torture. "What do you want from me?"

"I want you out of the way!" the queen shrieked, that booming voice again.

Erelah flinched but managed to stay clear of the bars.

"Let Leksander go. Tell him he needs to move on. Tell him you're not worthy of him."

All of it was true, but Erelah's dulled mind couldn't quite piece it together. Why was this of such concern to the Queen of the Summer Court? Was it that he bore her blood? Did she want so terribly for the treaty to renew? "I have tried," Erelah gasped out. And it was the truth. But Leksander never listened to her. Never paid her heed. Her eyes were drifting closed. She just needed to rest… a jolt of pain from one tip of her wing brought her awake.

The queen was still staring at her, fury on her face. "I will let you go, if you spurn him. Send him away. Break his heart into a million pieces. I'll put them back together again. I will make him my prince. My consort. My True Love. I will give him a child, and he will be *mine.*"

Her True Love? Erelah stared at the queen in horror. The queen had love of Leksander? And wished him for a mate? A struggle inside her felt like two angelings sparring, each striking with deadly intent with their blades. Because, on the one hand, this made perfect sense. A queen for a mate. A renewal of the treaty. The summer fae would protect the House of Smoke. Even if they were the sworn and loathsome enemies of angelkind, the Summer Court formed the treaty to begin with. They could strengthen and protect the House of Smoke once again.

How could she deny Leksander this?

And yet… and yet a deep and primal scream inside her was crying out, *No!*

"Then I shall have your blood on my floor," the queen hissed.

Erelah blinked, just now realizing she must have uttered that *No!* aloud.

The queen raised her hand, but before she could strike whatever blow she had planned, she stiffened, as if hearing a distant scream. Only Erelah wasn't screaming, and neither was anything else in the flowery and strange wonderland of the queen's throne room.

A moment later, the red-haired fae appeared behind the queen. "My lady," he said, voice strained. "Allow me. Please."

The queen's gaze whipped between her minion and Erelah in the cage. She seemed torn. Finally, she said to the red-haired fae, "Buy me a little time, Kalen. Then bring my beloved here."

The fae—Kalen—winced as though she had struck him, but then he turned and disappeared from the throne room.

The queen pointed a long finger at her. "You will *not* stand in my way."

Erelah pulled in a full breath and prepared herself to die.

Chapter Fourteen

WHEN KALEN APPEARED, LEKSANDER WAS CERTAIN HE'D strike first, ask questions later.

Leksander tensed and prepared to fight on the narrow rocky ledge of the weigh station—or take to the air if that gave him and the angeling at his back an advantage—but Kalen just demanded to know his business with the queen. When Leksander only told him he needed to speak to her, Kalen disappeared again, and Leksander couldn't be sure what would happen next.

He turned to Tajael. "What do you make of that?"

"I believe this Kalen has love of the queen that goes beyond the loyalty of a servant," Tajael observed dryly.

"He's her lover." Leksander brushed that aside. "But do you think he'll deliver the message? Or should I call the queen again?" The tension was riding him hard—Erelah could already be dead. He couldn't read that evil glint in Kalen's eyes.

"Wait." Tajael squinted at the space the fae had just occupied. "Kalen's turmoil was a thick soup of emotion on his face." He looked to Leksander. "He considers you a rival."

"Well, I did promise to mate with the queen." Leksander grimaced. "Not that it should matter. She already consorts with Kalen, and the king doesn't care. I'm not sure normal rules apply in the Summer Court."

Tajael's eyebrows lifted. "Oh, they definitely have rules. You should know that, prince of the House of Smoke. Your ancestor helped the prior queen break one of the most important ones."

Leksander's eyes narrowed. "She had a child outside the royal lineage."

"She *loved* outside the royal lineage," Tajael said, pointedly. "The child was simply a product of it. As you know, there was no accident in the birth of that child—it was an intentional slap in the face of the king."

"And now Nyssa wants to do the same with me." Leksander frowned. "Is this some kind of trap, Tajael? Is Nyssa just trying to provoke the king into killing me? And along with me, all of the House of Smoke?" His gut hollowed out with that thought. Not that he wanted to mate with Nyssa, but if it came to that… was it all a mistake?

"The fae are liars and deceitful, through-and-through," Tajael said. "But it's a rather elaborate deception if that's what it is. And Kalen's reaction to you… it's more than just a concern that the queen will take another lover."

Leksander eyes widened. "He loves her."

"A rather unrequited love," Tajael agreed. "His hatred of you would be unbounded if you actually mated with the queen. I would watch your back in this, Leksander."

He shook his head. "My only concern is for Erelah and getting her free."

A slow smile spread on Tajael's face. "Spoken like True Love."

Then a pop in the air announced Kalen's return. Before Leksander could even turn to face him, the queen's lover grabbed hold of his shoulder from behind and wrenched him through time and space. When the world stopped shifting, Leksander glimpsed the hanging vines of the queen's throne room, but then Kalen shoved him face-first in the grass carpet.

"Kalen!" the queen's voice boomed admonishment.

He backed off as Leksander climbed to his feet. The red-haired servant of the queen was nothing if not obedient, but his face seethed with a fury that would melt Leksander into a pile of dragon goo if Nyssa let him off the leash. That, more than anything else, convinced him that Kalen was madly in love with the queen—which would be a serious problem if they mated. One more reason for Leksander not to let it get that far.

He brushed grass from his pants and turned to Nyssa, who was across the room, next to the throne and a strange golden cage that looked like it had crash-landed. "Nyssa, I need to know if—" But the words stopped dead in his throat when he saw the body lying at Nyssa's feet.

A body with white wings.

He lurched across the throne room, shoving vines out of his way and nearly tripping over some cluster of flowers. *"What have you done?"* he roared, but then he was too busy falling to his knees next to Erelah's body to listen to the queen's excuses for the horror of this. Erelah's beautiful white wings were branded with stripes of black char. Her feet were swollen and angry red, and the number of red welts across her body... Leksander sobbed and cupped his hand to her cheek, where a burn mark had disfigured her face. Tears glassed his eyes. "No, no, no." But then he choked on his own horror.

"She is not dead, dragon prince." Nyssa's voice was cool behind him, and the words had to fight through a haze in his brain before he could hear them.

When he did, he just blinked then reached out with his own fae senses to check—the queen was right. Erelah was alive, only… sleeping. Horribly burned and broken and abused, but not irreparably so. He lurched up from the floor and whirled on Nyssa.

"Why would you do this?" he demanded. The urge to strangle her or blast her with dragonfire or *something* was almost impossible to contain… but he did. Because there was no other way to get Erelah out of the queen's clutches, healed, and safely away.

"I will let her go if you stay, Leksander." Her even tone of voice, as if this were just some business transaction, was driving him mad.

"I told you two days—"

"You had no intention of honoring that." The queen's voice hiked up. "We both know that."

Erelah's broken body on the floor drew his gaze like a horror he couldn't look away from. "You did this to force my hand." Guilt and sickness twisted his stomach.

Nyssa eased closer to him and cupped his cheek with her palm. Pleasure rushed through him, a nauseating mix with the horror stringing his body tight. He wrenched his face away and glared at her.

The queen dropped her hand, left hovering in the air. "She does *not* love you," she cried out, her voice suddenly bitter and angry.

Kalen appeared by her side. "My lady—"

She held a hand up to stop him without looking at him.

He slunk back, stepping away from the queen and falling silent.

Nyssa's violet eyes were still trained on Leksander. "I tormented her. Asked her if she *could* love you. If she would *ever* love you, and do you know what she said, Leksander?"

He shook his head. It didn't matter what Erelah said, but he still didn't want to hear it.

"I have love of him as a friend." Nyssa's voice arched high, an imitation of Erelah's innocence, but the sneer in it tore into him.

"It doesn't matter," he whispered. He knew this already. It hurt, but it wouldn't stop him from getting Erelah free.

"Of course, it matters," Nyssa said angrily. "Love is *all* that matters."

Leksander squinted at her. "What will it take for you to let her go?"

"I told you already."

"You can't force me to love you, Nyssa."

"I don't need you to love me!" Her voice hiked up again, and it was a lie. Leksander could hear her neediness.

"You think if we mate that I'll love you," Leksander said, each word wrenching his stomach a little tighter. "That's not going to happen." Despite all his cool calculations, despite his lofty ideals of loving any woman who might give him a son to fulfill the treaty, by sheer dint that *that woman* would have True Love *for him*... he knew now that he could never love someone else. He loved Erelah. He had loved her from nearly the moment they met, all those decades ago, and that was an immutable fact of his heart. It wouldn't change even if he had found Erelah dead on the queen's throne room floor. It was an essential part of him now.

"Your love is not necessary for us to mate," Nyssa said. There was a torment in her violet eyes that Leksander had not seen before. "The king of the court has no love of me and never will. And I cannot love him in return. And that loveless queendom is *not enough!* I've suffered it, all these long millennium, all in a Court bound by the torrid love of my mother and the treaty she forged with it. But I deserve *more.* I deserve a love of my own!" Her voice was booming painfully loud now. "I may be bound by law and tradition to a loveless king, but I *will* have a consort of my own to love, even if you do not love me back, prince of the House of Smoke. And you know you can never fulfill the treaty with *her!*" She flung an accusatory finger at Erelah's limp body. "She is an angeling, and thus stupid and vain for her own perfection. She can *never* love you. *But I can.* You *need* me!" She had stepped closer again, the passion alight in her eyes making it clear she meant every word.

And she wasn't wrong, not really. For the first time, Leksander believed he understood *why* the queen was willing to mate with him. It was sad and wrong and completely fucked up, but he understood. He wouldn't give up the love he had for Erelah for anything, even though she didn't love him in return… and the queen only wanted that, and the possibility of more. After ten thousand years of a life empty of love, he could understand her desperation.

She edged closer and gripped his arm, keeping away from the flesh-on-flesh contact. "You *need* me, Leksander," she said, low and tight. "We need *each other.* I'll let the angeling go if you just come to me and let me give you everything you need. I promise my love will be True. I will give you a child, and we will fulfill the treaty together." Her hand kneaded the muscles on his arm, as if to remind him of the pleasures that awaited him, if only he said yes.

He was tempted, only because of the pleading look in her eyes. It was the most *human* thing he'd ever seen in her. Then he pictured five hundred years of power plays in the bedroom—the ones that turned her on but left him cold—and he doubted he could endure it. Plus that was a lot of time for someone like Kalen—or another fae infinitely more powerful than Leksander—to slip a dagger into him. No, if Erelah could never love him, then he'd be better off finding a human female and secreting her away to mate and have a dragonling. This fucking around with the politics of the Summer Court was too dangerous.

But how to get the queen to release him? When the need in her eyes for love would surely translate into rage if it wasn't met?

The sound of something tightening behind him made him turn. Kalen stood with his hands clenched, rigidly staring at the point where Nyssa's hand gripped Leksander's arm. The noise was a grinding of magic that seemed to come from his clenched fists.

Kalen.

Leksander turned back to Nyssa. "Send Kalen away."

"What?" Nyssa blinked, his words seeming to jar her. "He's only—"

"I cannot stand his presence," Leksander growled out, as if he were jealous of Kalen. "Send him out of my sight!"

She jolted and flicked a hand at Kalen, shooing him away.

The rage on the fae's face was missed by Nyssa—her gaze had never wavered from Leksander's—but Kalen twisted and disappeared.

Leksander gripped the queen by the shoulders. "Do you not see him, Nyssa?"

"What?" She looked dazed, like his words made no sense.

"Kalen loves you." He stated it boldly, hoping that might break through.

"He does not matter—"

"Do you want love, Nyssa?" he demanded, squeezing her shoulders harder. "Do you want someone who would do anything for you? Lay down his life. Frustrate his own needs. Bring another lover to your bed, if that's what you desire? Surely, you have to see it."

She twisted out of his hold. "Kalen is simply…" But she stalled out, and he knew he was closing in on it.

"Tell me he hasn't filled your bed."

"That's of no concern—"

"*Tell me* he hasn't been there every time you had an itch that needed scratching. A frustration that needed venting. A loneliness that ached just a little more than you could bear." He was full-on guessing now, but by the wide-eyed look on her face, he was hitting home.

"He's a servant. Good only for…" But the look on her face was uncertain now.

"Why would you want someone like me?" Leksander pressed. "Someone forced into your bed? When you could have someone who would give his life for you?"

Resistance finally surged up in her eyes. "He's not like you! He's not royalty and a *beast* the way you are. There's no…" She gestured to Leksander's body with a flailing of hands. "There's no essence of wildness, the kind which drew my mother in."

"You are *not* your mother." Leksander grabbed hold of her shoulders again, and her eyes were wide, staring up at him. "She nearly broke your Court seeking True Love. But you've got True Love staring you in the face!"

Her mouth fell open, then she drew back from him. "He is a lesser in my court. He is unworthy of the love of a queen."

"And he knows that," Leksander said, nodding. He fairly loathed Kalen and all his sneers and threats and rage, but he couldn't help feeling sympathy for a man in love with a woman hopelessly out of his league. Leksander knew that feeling all too well. "Open your eyes, Nyssa. And believe that True Love has a power and magic all its own. Your mother proved that. Your Court has abided by that idea for millennia. Let it work *for* you this time, instead of against you."

He could see the words working their magic on her. But still, she was frowning. "I don't know if I can love him."

"Maybe you can't," Leksander conceded, although it felt dangerous to admit that so close to convincing her. "But if you *could...* think of it, Nyssa. Think of what you could have with him. I will never love you as he does."

And that did it. He could see it by the way her eyes opened not with horror or surprise, but with hope. "You think it's possible?"

"My House is ruled by Love," he said with a small smile. "You'd be surprised by the miracles I've seen True Love conduct."

She gave him a small nod, and suddenly, she looked vulnerable. Shaken. Awed by the possibility, maybe, that she could have a True Love of her own. Leksander knew that was how he felt every damn time he looked at Erelah.

"Let me take her, Nyssa." He gestured to Erelah's still inert body, his heart wrenching again at the sight. "Let me take the woman I love and at least try to see if I can win her love in return. Even if I can't, at least I'll have given my best to the only thing that really matters in this world."

Nyssa scowled, but it looked as much to hold back tears as anything. He had a strange lightness in his heart. Like somehow this was how it was meant to be—the fae queen finding her True Love just as he was finding his. Without a word, Nyssa held out a hand and conjured a pink butterfly-sprite, the kind that flitted around her throne room.

As she held it, fluttering above her palm, she quietly said, "Kalen, I have need of you."

Her lover instantly appeared by her side. He threw an uncertain scowl at Leksander and noted Erelah still lying in the grass, then looked to Nyssa for her bidding. She turned and looked at him, peering at him like she'd never really seen him before. Which Leksander guessed was probably the sum of it.

Her stare seemed to unnerve Kalen. He flicked an angry look at Leksander, then dipped his head to her, his expression becoming alarmed. "Is my queen all right?"

She nodded. "Take the dragon and angeling back to his realm. They're not to be harmed. Then return to me, Kalen. I'll have need of you then."

He frowned, and Leksander had to rub the back of his hand across his mouth to keep from smiling. "As you wish, my queen," Kalen said.

Nyssa turned to Leksander and held the pink sprite out to him. "Use this to wake her when you're ready."

He hesitated but held out his hand. The misty butterfly condensed into a tiny pink angel in his palm. He slipped it into his pocket and gave her a small smile. "Thank you."

She waved it away as if she were embarrassed. Leksander sure as hell wasn't going to push his luck. He'd convinced the summer queen to conduct her own search for True Love, and not *with him*, so he would make haste to beat a retreat before any of that changed. He hurried to Erelah's side, where Kalen was waiting, a confused concern still clouding his face. Kalen placed a hand on both, then wrenched them away from the throne room.

When Leksander's senses came back, Erelah was lying on the rocky ledge of the weigh station with him and Kalen kneeling next to her. The wards kept them out, so this was as close as Kalen—or Erelah, for that matter—could get to the keep.

Tajael was still there, waiting for them. *"Holy angels of light,"* he whispered softly upon seeing Erelah's body.

Kalen snarled at him and disappeared an instant later, no doubt in a hurry to return to his queen.

"She's alive." Tajael's voice was still filled with wonder, but he hung back, as if afraid to encroach on them.

"And I can heal her." Leksander's heart was torn anew as he bent over Erelah's torture-wracked body.

"Do you need assistance?" Tajael asked, his voice strangely soft.

"No." Leksander's gaze was fixed on Erelah's beautiful but scorched face. He dug out the waking-sprite from his pocket. "I can wake her with this."

"Then, I'll leave you to it," Tajael said in that soft voice again.

When Leksander looked up, he was gone. Which was just as well. Leksander placed the tiny pink angel on Erelah's breast, just above her heart, and the thing turned into mist which then sunk into her body. His breath caught, and he prayed to magic the queen hadn't slipped some kind of evil sprite to him instead. But Erelah stirred on the rocky ground and gave a small moan of pain. He quickly set to work, slicing open his palm for a fresh dose of healing dragon blood and summoning his runes to heal her that way. He gently laid hands on every scorch mark, every angry burn welt, and slowly healed the torture wounds his beloved had endured on his behalf.

Healing her body might be all she would want from him. But when she awoke, he would do everything in his power to convince her that loving him was exactly what was meant to be.

She owned his heart regardless.

Chapter Fifteen

Her heart raced with it—because this pleasure came not from slaying demons but from light whispers of touch all over her body. Even with her eyes closed, she knew that was wrong. Something was very, very wrong. She struggled to wake out of the dream, but her eyelids stayed stubbornly stuck shut as the pleasure continued, evincing small moans from her as each touch brought another pulse. Her wings, her back, her feet… there was nowhere the warmth of that touch didn't travel up and down her body. She vaguely noticed, as she swam closer to full consciousness, that the ground was hard and cool and unevenly pointed underneath her. The touches, by contrast, were warm and soft and zinged with pleasure. She prickled with pain everywhere, as well, but the touches made the pain recede and layered over a soothing blanket of pleasure on top.

The heat of those touches lasted long after the source had moved on to other places.

Finally, she felt air pulling sharply into her lungs, dragging her awake enough to blink open her eyes and squint at the figure holding her hand, palm up.

Leksander.

She struggled to lift up from the rocky ledge she was lying on. It was the weigh station outside the House of Smoke. How in all the Dominions did she get here?

Leksander let go of her hand, but then he cupped both her cheeks in his large, warm hands. She managed to sit up, but he held her like that, eyes shining, a smile broad across his face, as he flushed that same pleasure into her, the kind that mingled her angel power with his dragon and fae magic. It was like when they kissed before—that one time which she vowed never to repeat—only this time her mouth hung open, her entire body buzzed, and she was breathless with him just holding her skin-to-skin on her face. The flush on his cheeks, the dilation of his eyes—she could see them so wide and ice-blue with him this close— all of it said he felt this strange magical connection, too. The one that was coiling a tight knot of need deep in her belly.

Then, suddenly, he released her.

She nearly toppled over to the ground.

He braced her by grabbing her upper arms and holding her upright. "Whoa," he said. "Maybe you should lie back down."

Lie down? With Leksander? He meant it literally, not figuratively, as in having sexual contact, but her body was pulsing with his magic *everywhere.* Lying down seemed precipitously unwise, like jumping off a cliff when your wings were clipped and hoping you will not crash at the bottom.

"I am fine." She waved off his touch then noticed her own arm. It was flushed pink, like his cheeks, and a memory poked at her. *The burns.* They were gone. She looked up at Leksander with wide eyes.

"I've been healing you," he said, a little breathless. "It took awhile." He didn't seem like he minded—almost the opposite. Like he was apologizing for enjoying it so much.

Erelah inched away from him, protectively gaining distance, lest she ask him to keep "healing" her more with those gentle touches. But that small movement made his expression pinch in, like it was causing him pain.

"Thank you," she rushed out, holding a hand out to reassure him but then bringing it back in before he might touch her. "Thank you for healing me." She had to be *swimming* in fae and dragon magic now. As she checked her wings, which were still extended, and her legs and arms, every last burn was gone, but there were still smears of Leksander's blood. How much did he use to heal her?

He was sitting on his heels, kneeling in front of her, waiting. Patient.

Then she remembered. "The queen. How did you…" She frowned, hard. What did Leksander do to gain her freedom? And why did he come for her? She was afraid she knew all too well the reason, if not the exact method.

"I convinced the queen to let you go." His eyes were dancing with a held-in laugh, as if it were a joke about which only he and the queen were privy.

Her heart ached with that thought, and it truly shouldn't. She shouldn't try to keep Leksander apart from the queen, even though she was fae. Erelah dropped her gaze to the rocky ground next to her folded-up legs. "The queen has love of you." When he didn't respond, she looked up. "What did you give her to secure my release?" she couldn't help asking, even though she didn't want to know, not really.

He smiled, and it seemed full of genuine pleasure. Maybe all the light touches had affected him, too. "I convinced her to pursue her own True Love."

She frowned again. "But she wished *you* to love her. She would do anything for it."

"She's not the one I love, Erelah."

Then she had to look away. Because his eyes lit up as he said that. Because this had all gone wrong. She was supposed to fly away, go into seclusion, have her Penance... not ruin any chance Leksander had with the summer queen. He wasn't supposed to rescue her. Or heal her. Or look upon her like he wished a repeat of that dangerous kiss in the throne room of his keep.

"Erelah," he said, and suddenly his voice was closer. He had moved to sit in front of her, legs also crossed. Their knees nearly touched—hers were bare, but his were safely covered by his trousers. She had a new and deep appreciation for why humans and dragons wore such substantial clothing. When any exposed skin could be cause for such pleasureful contact...

He dipped his head to catch her gaze. "I convinced Nyssa to go after her own True Love because that's what it took to get you out of there. She told me that love was all that really mattered in the end, and she was right. But somehow, she hadn't seen the True Love that was right in her own Court all along."

Erelah winced because it wasn't hard, not with that look on his face, to know his meaning. "I know you have love of me, Leksander, but—"

"But you can't love me. I know." He was still smiling, gently, at her.

Her eyes widened. "Then why did you..." She gestured with empty hands at the healing he had done to her body, the very idea that he would risk himself, his House, and the treaty, all to save her from a Penance she deserved.

"Why did I rescue you?" he asked, his smile growing. "Why did I risk the wrath of a fae queen just to get you out of there? Why did I heal every wound on your body that I could find?" His smile settled into a soft smirk. Then he picked up her hand, which was lying in her lap, and stroked her fingers with his thumb. That same rush of pleasure moved through them then rippled through her body, singing with all the other recently healed spots which held his dragon and fae magic. They were like a choir all around her body, trilling together. "I'll admit that I was probably more thorough on the healing than necessary," he said. "This feeling when I touch you, Erelah… it intoxicates me." He breathed out the last words.

She gasped and drew her hand away.

Again, that look of disappointment on his face made her want to reach out to him.

"I understand," he said, even though sadness was laced in this voice. "You tried to tell me before, but I didn't really get it. Tajael explained. How you've never had someone love you before. Not even your own mother. You were taken away to live with Angels, and my love for you has to be strange. And overwhelming. And possibly something you'll never understand." He leaned forward, getting closer to her, but clasping his hands so she needn't fear he might touch her again. "But the reason I needed so save you from Nyssa's grasp has nothing to do with whether you will love me or not… and entirely to do with the fact that *I* love *you*."

Erelah just blinked. Her heart lurched and then raced, trying to run away from the love that was plain in Leksander's eyes. She couldn't deny he felt it—that was *truth,* and she was committed to truth in all things—but she could dispute the wisdom. Dissuade him so he would find someone who *could* mate with him.

"We cannot… this isn't something that can work, Leksander," she said, trying her hardest to be gentle because she didn't want to see that look of disappointment or pain on his face again. Ever. "How can we be sure the mating is even possible? Would you seal me with your mark? What if an angeling cannot be sealed?"

He seemed to fight a smile, but she was dead serious. "I've just infused you with enough dragon blood that I'm pretty sure you're half dragon already."

She scowled. "I am not."

His grin broke out. "We can change that."

"I am serious, Leksander."

The smile fell away from his face. "So am I."

That intense look on his face felt almost as powerful as the touch of his healing hands. She looked away again, flicking at a pebble on the rocky ground near her knee. "Even if we could mate, how can we make a baby between dragons and angels?" She looked back at him, giving her best serious expression. Because all depended on this. "I've seen how hard it is for a human to bring a dragonling to term. How much harder for a baby with such disparate forces? The angel and fae within it would fight, constantly."

He edged forward again, letting his hands fall close to her knees, but not touching. "Rosalyn carried a demon for almost the entire term. And she was only a witch. *You're* an angel."

"Half angel," she said, annoyed that he wrenched that out of her.

He smiled, gently. "And your human half will be

strengthened by your angel power. If your mother could carry you, Erelah, I'm convinced you could carry a child of mine."

He spoke the words with such tenderness and conviction, it threatened to tear her in two. "But… but…" Air was becoming difficult to force into her lungs. "But the baby—what would it be? Fae and angel and dragonling? What about the treaty? Would this hybrid baby be enough for—"

"Shhh," he said, taking up her hand once more and effectively cutting off all her words. "None of that matters," he said with a soft smile. "None of it… unless you love me. And not just the love of a friend, Erelah. A True Love. And I know that's the hardest part of all. I know it because Tajael told me. He spoke of how it was for angelings, how hard it was, and I believe him. But I also know it because I know that *if* you loved me, if somehow by some miracle you were able to actually love me, well then… everything else is possible."

Air was laboring in her chest now. All the wounds from her supposed Penance in the queen's chamber were gone, whisked away by Leksander's dragon blood and fae magic, and her body was buzzing with the pleasure of his hand touching hers. Now all this talk of loving, when that wasn't a thing she could even think of doing, was making her more light-headed.

But then he gently pulled her closer, tugging on her hand. "All we need to worry about," he whispered, soft and low, as he leaned in, "the only thing that matters… is finding out if love is something you can feel for me." His clear blue eyes were staring into hers, and she felt that connection like a tether between their souls. There was no possibility of her looking away. Or speaking. Or even breathing.

Then his gaze dropped to her lips, and he leaned forward, seeking them.

This time, his kiss would not take her by surprise. This time, she knew exactly his intent. She should run away or push him back or, at a minimum, put a hand to his chest and stop his advance, but she did none of those things. She let him lean forward and press his lips to hers, and only then, could she breathe again. A gasp as he touched her. He pulled back slightly, released her hand, and cupped her cheek instead. Then with an aching and deliberate slowness—for how else could she explain her need for him to go *faster*—he leaned in to kiss her again.

Her heart thrummed in her ears like a hundred beating wings. His touch was feather-soft at first, but then his lips moved urgently against hers. She grabbed at him without realizing, but suddenly her hands were gripping his shoulders, bringing him closer. A rumbling sound in his chest tightened something deep and low in her belly, and she opened her mouth to his, inviting him in. The rumble moved up to his chest and turned into a moan as his tongue darted into her, hot and probing and insistent. She moved with him, her tongue matching his, her movements a mirror at first, then taking the lead.

Always, when Leksander was near, the fae in his blood brought a kind of exciting edginess to her body, a sharpness to her mind. As if he were just a little dangerous, just a little *wild*. Now, with his fae blood infusing her wounds, and his tongue probing her mouth, and his hands wrapping urgently in her hair, that edge of danger ignited in her a burning need for more.

"I have…" she panted as she kissed him. "A need. Such *need.*" She whimpered the last of that, and Leksander growled a possessive sound that transfixed her and set her body even more on fire with this indescribable *need* that she felt only he could fulfill.

His arm wrapped around her waist, holding her tight, while his lips left hers and traveled along her jaw. She automatically tilted her head back, giving him better access, and her eyes fell shut.

"Oh God, Erelah," he panted against her skin. He reached her neck, and his lips there sent shock waves that reverberated around her body but seemed to focus most between her legs. The wildness—that edge inside her— grew sharper, and she grabbed at him with more power, pulling him harder against her neck.

"More," she gasped because even as he kissed her there, it wasn't enough. But her hands flailed at his shoulders. She didn't know how to do what her body was screaming for—what that wildness inside her was demanding—and that just escalated her frustration into a writhing ball of *need* inside her. *"More,* Leksander..." The words made her mouth ache, and that tension low in her belly grew painfully tight. "Give me *more."*

He groaned into the flesh of her neck and grabbed hard onto her bottom, pulling her body up and flush against his. His erect penis was trapped between them, and her pulse throbbed at every point of her body where he'd healed her, but especially between her legs, where she was sure he had not. His other hand wrapped tightly in her hair, and suddenly his mouth was consuming her—tongue hard and demanding, lips soft but made of steel. Her hands finally found purpose in ripping the shirt from his shoulders, grabbing hold on each side and rending the fabric apart. That left nothing but bare skin and multiplied the effect of their touch by a hundredfold, surging all at once. She cried out and pushed him back to the ground, needing to pin him while she gave her hands free roam over the expanse of muscles on his shoulders and his chest. His eyes went wide as she took liberties, straddling him, so the heat between her legs ground against the rock-hardness of his body. His *maleness* was an intoxication, a fever dream she had once and forgot. She wanted his hard edge to carve through her, cleaving her as she dragged her hands down his body. She panted as though breath no longer belonged to her, and her hands craved to stroke him.

"Erelah!" Only the terror in his eyes stopped her hazed groping.

She jerked, a chill running through her. Had she hurt him?

But he wasn't looking at her… he was looking *past her.*

"Your wings." It was a gasp of horror.

Her head whipped to the side to look. Holy angels of —*no!*

Her wings. They were black as midnight.

She flung herself up and away from Leksander's body, screeching as she hurtled into the air. She twisted to see, spinning in the air, trying to claw at the infernal black feathers as if they belonged to some attacking vapor… *but they were hers.*

A howl of pain and shame and horror worked from deep in her belly straight up and out of her mouth… *and she screamed and screamed and screamed.* An angelsong so bright and so powerful it shook loose rocks that tumbled down and rolled to where Leksander lay on his back, thrown down by her unhinged passions.

She gaped at him, so beautiful and alluring, and all she wanted was to ravage him. Take him. Sin again and again and again in an unending orgy of Lust. She wanted to shatter what shreds of Chastity she had left until she was completely turned.

She was Shadow.

Her own Fall had come in a heady rush, and she could do nothing any longer without Sin. She screeched all the pain and sorrow there was in her body, expending it in sound and despair. Then she pumped her wings away from him and twisted to hurtle herself far from this man, this beautiful man, this overpoweringly tempting man…

Forever.

Chapter Sixteen

Leksander thought he knew.

He thought he understood heartbreak. He thought he knew what it was like to feel pain inside your heart and mind and soul that could turn you inside out.

He knew nothing.

He lay, frozen, on the rocky ledge for a time without measure.

What had he done?

He didn't move. Or speak. Or even breathe, until his lungs were on fire with the need to do so, and he relented. Horror held him captive, pinned to the rock… right until a pop in the air made his heart seize so hard, he thought it might kill him.

It was Tajael.

His face was a picture of panic. "No," he gasped from his spot at the end of the rocky ledge. "I felt… a shockwave through magic space…" His face crumpled. "Please tell me she didn't…"

Leksander lurched to his feet. *"What happened to her?"* he demanded as he raged across the narrow ledge. He grabbed hold of the angeling by his flimsy toga and shouted in his face. *"Her wings were black!"*

The last shred of hope left Tajael's face, and it folded into despair. "She has fallen."

Leksander shoved him away and stumbled back. "Fallen."

Tajael didn't explain further, just bent his head and wept silent tears. But he didn't have to. Leksander knew what had happened. He knew what he had done.

He had tempted her with his love and his kisses and his soft promises...

And he had broken her.

Leksander and Erelah's story continues in…

MARKED BY A DRAGON

(Fallen Immortals 8)

Grab Marked by a Dragon today!

Subscribe to Alisa's newsletter

for new releases and giveaways

http://smarturl.it/AWsubscribeBARDS

About the Author

Alisa Woods lives in the Midwest with her husband and family, but her heart will always belong to the beaches and mountains where she grew up. She writes sexy paranormal romances about complicated men and the strong women who love them. Her books explore the struggles we all have, where we resist—and succumb to—our most tempting vices as well as our greatest desires. No matter the challenge, Alisa firmly believes that hearts can mend and love will triumph over all.

www.AlisaWoodsAuthor.com